D0021181

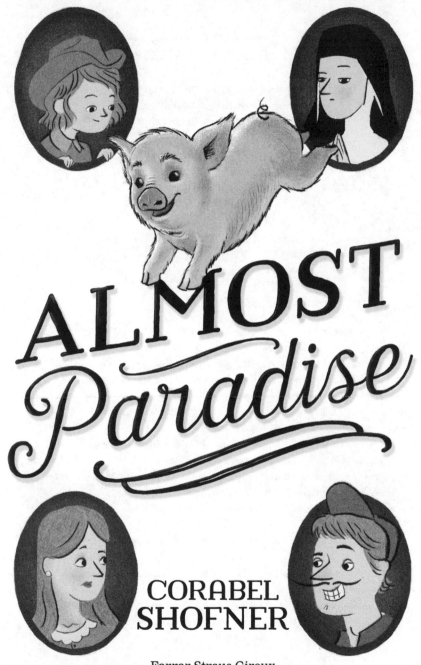

ALMOST Paradise

CORABEL SHOFNER

Farrar Straus Giroux
New York

Farrar Straus Giroux Books for Young Readers
An imprint of Macmillan Publishing Group, LLC
175 Fifth Avenue, New York, NY 10010

mackids.com

Library of Congress Cataloging-in-Publication Data

Names: Shofner, Corabel, author.
Title: Almost paradise : a novel / Corabel Shofner.
Description: First edition. | New York : Farrar, Straus and Giroux, 2017. |
    Summary: When twelve-year-old Ruby's mother goes to jail, Ruby finds her
    Aunt Eleanor, an ornery nun with some dark secrets, who Ruby hopes will
    help free her mother.
Identifiers: LCCN 2016038518 (print) | LCCN 2017018123 (ebook) | ISBN
    9780374303792 (ebook) | ISBN 9780374303785 (hardback)
Subjects: | CYAC: Mothers and daughters—Fiction. | Single-parent
    families—Fiction. | Aunts—Fiction. | Nuns—Fiction. |
    Prisoners—Fiction. | Cancer—Fiction. | BISAC: JUVENILE FICTION / Action
    & Adventure / General. | JUVENILE FICTION / Law & Crime.
Classification: LCC PZ7.1.S5178 (ebook) | LCC PZ7.1.S5178 Alm 2017 (print) |
    DDC [Fic]—dc23
LC record available at https://lccn.loc.gov/2016038518

Our books may be purchased in bulk for promotional, educational, or
business use. Please contact your local bookseller or the Macmillan
Corporate and Premium Sales Department at (800) 221-7945 ext. 5442 or
by e-mail at MacmillanSpecialMarkets@macmillan.com.

ellee

*For Belmont, who told me stories before we knew
words; for Debra, who is my fierce protector; and
for Martin, who gave me a life of love and these
children: Alex, Markham, and Jesse*

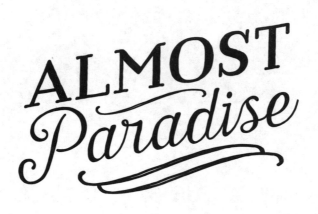

I WOKE UP ALONE IN THE BACKSEAT OF THE Catfish's car. That was my mother's boyfriend. Don't get me started on the Catfish. His real name was Carl but I called him the Catfish, because that's exactly what he looked like. The distance between his eyes was enormous, and he had skinny lips and a pointy mustache. If I'd been older when he came around, I never would have allowed him into our lives. But honest to God, I had no entire clue how to get rid of him once he was wedged into our family. You may as well know, Mother was no help at all, but don't hold that against her: she'd been real fragile since my father died, which was before I was born. I was still inside Mother at the time and his shooting death actually made me come out.

Anyway, Catfish wasn't in the car and neither was my mother. The sun was all over me, and I was tangled up in the blanket, staring up at the ceiling—thumbtacks held up the saggy material. And you know, at first I didn't even wonder where I was. I mean, I knew I was in the Catfish's car, but to think outside the car would be like wondering where my planet was in the universe.

I sat up to look for Mom. She was just outside, sitting on an upturned log by a burning campfire, watching coffee perk into the glass knob on top of a metal pot. A lady holding a carton of milk sat on the log beside Mother. I thought she was the nurse from school, with those blond curls all around her face. But then I realized that I'd never seen her before.

It still hadn't hit me how much we were not home—really, really not at home. I rested my cheek on the window and watched Mother watch the coffee brew. She sat real dainty, with her feet and knees together. My mother was always a pretty person, even in the morning. Her hair was thick and wavy around the shoulders of her favorite dress. Pale pink flowers, green leaves with an occasional bug; she'd replaced missing buttons at least ten times. She kept herself real clean too, which was something I could stand to learn.

What's more, she was calm, being outside and all, so I knew Catfish was nearby. Mother's almost like those agora-something people on TV, the ones who can't go out of the house, but she's not mentally ill. There's no medical words ending in *-oids* or *-icks* for what she was. It's just that, after my father died, she stayed inside so much that she forgot how to get along in the world. It all seemed like chaos to her, she said. The Catfish got her to go outside more, but so what? We didn't need him.

Speaking of outside, we were surrounded by those big RVs, tents, and pop-up campers, all under the trees. It was organized, somehow, like an outdoor hotel, and then I started to think—*Where the heck are we?* I went to sleep at home and woke up in some kind of vagabond camp.

Inside, the car was all packed up—that should have told me something. It was stuffed full of my toys and workbooks, clothes, and two horrible orange lamps. Looked like all our belongings, but that didn't upset me right away. I only got upset when I tried to get out of the car and put my foot down on a flimsy box. I knew what it was as soon as I felt the cardboard crush. My heart sank.

My birthday cake! I had stepped on my birthday cake. The one I had bought for myself at the grocery store; the one my friend Bunny and I were supposed to share at home that afternoon for my twelfth birthday. (Mother could never celebrate my birthday, because of Father and all.) But I couldn't figure out what my cake was doing there on the backseat floor of the Catfish's car. I pulled the box up on my lap and lifted the busted top.

Inside it said: —PY—DAY—UBY.

I cried big tears. I was no crybaby but I was so surprised to wreck my own name that the tears just leaked out. HAP and BIRTH could fall by the wayside, but losing the R from RUBY—now that hurt; it hurt bad. I knew from the Bible that when somebody got a name change, God was about to let it rip. So I knew then, just sitting and looking at that UBY, that even though it was only my twelfth birthday, my life was turning upside down.

I opened the car door, swung my feet out, and walked over to Mother. She turned slowly from the fire to look at me. She was pleased to see me; I could always tell by her eyes, and the warm light there she saved for me alone. "Where are we?" I pulled on the elastic waist of my pajamas and let it pop. "Aren't I supposed to be in school today?"

The lady with the blond curls could tell I was confused and needed to talk to my mother, so instead of talking, she politely turned away and stirred the fire with a long stick.

Mother tilted her head and gestured to the woods and the campers all around us. She had this way of looking at ordinary things like she had never seen them before.

I got right in front of Mother and touched her cheek. The fire warmed my back. "How far are we from home, Mom? Do you know?"

She sighed. "Oh—about . . ."

"How long did we drive last night? Do you remember? Were you awake?"

She glanced over at the car as if it might tell her. Then she said, "The sun came up behind us. It was lovely. I almost woke you up to see it."

All night traveling in the car! We could have been in

China, for all I knew. "Mother," I said slowly, "where is the Catfish taking us?"

She nodded peacefully, then touched her lips. "Hollywood. It's in California."

I could not believe my ears. The Catfish probably thought he was going to get into movies or music. That was just like him, buying lottery tickets and gambling on any other fool thing that popped into his mind. He'd lay good money on whether the sun would come up and somehow he'd lose. The main problem with Catfish was he'd always been too good for his own life; he was always looking for a better place. And once he got going on one of his big ideas, it was near about impossible to slow his motor down.

"Where is he now?" I asked.

"Down there making friends, I suppose." She made a hand gesture like a fairy princess spreading stardust, then poured us each a cup of coffee.

TWO

*I*OUGHT TO SAY SOMETHING HERE ABOUT MY own self and the way I was back home, before they dragged me off on that horrible, horrible journey.

My name is Ruby Clyde Henderson and I am not stupid. What's more, I look like a boy, even at my age—I am skinny, and as my mother says, *flat as a pancake*. So when I want, I tell people my name is Clyde, and when I don't want, it's Ruby. Some don't even believe I'm a girl, with my hair being so short. It's funny, people tell you not to lie, but they hardly ever want to hear the truth. If you try to tell it, they call you a liar. *Liar, liar, pants on fire.* But if you lie, they believe you.

Back home there was this little blockheaded boy, new to school, and he actually pulled my pants down, wanting to prove that I was one of his kind. What he saw so surprised him that he laughed out loud, braying like a donkey. So I knocked him down—I'm good at that—and I sat on him. I'm good at that too. Then I snatched a sweat bee off the clover and shoved it in that boy's mouth and pinched his puffy lips closed until he fainted flat out.

I was in trouble with Mr. Upchurch, who had been principal since before the school was built. That man gave me the willies. And, of course, we called him Mr. Upchuck behind his back. His eyeglasses caught and reflected light, so you couldn't ever see his eyeballs. And what's worse than a grown man with no visible eyes?

I took my place in his "bad child's circle." We never got to sit down in Mr. Upchuck's office. He'd taped off a circle on the floor for us. It was supposed to make us feel squirmy. But I liked standing in the circle because I'd heard that if you put a rope around your tent when you were camping out, snakes couldn't get to you. So I always imagined the masking tape was rope, and that it kept Mr. Upchuck from getting his fangs in me. I had to stand in that circle for an hour just for beating up the little blockhead, but I would have done it again.

You'd think I didn't have any friends, after hearing a story like that. And I'm ashamed to tell it on myself—it makes me sound like a bully, which I'm not. Bullies pick on weak people. What fun is that? I only pick on bullies. Which means that most of my friends are weak people, which I like. They're much more interesting. I mean, bullies are all alike, really. That's why I beat them up.

What's more, I have a gift and talent. I don't know which it is, really—gift or talent—so I call it both. It is this: I am a healer. I do it with my hands. I haven't cured any cancers or brain tumors, not yet. I haven't cured any blindness or leprosies either. And to tell the truth, I haven't even cured a common cold, not yet. But that doesn't mean I won't one day.

For now, though, I can make people stop crying. And that's a God-given gift . . . and talent.

Whenever children back home got hurt on the playground, I'd lay my hands on them and they'd stop crying. The nurse was my friend, and she let me help her; told me I was her best student. (That's why she asked the bee-stung bully boy if he wanted me to help. He hadn't heard about that side of my personality, so you can imagine! When he heard my name, he flew up off her table and ran flat into the wall.)

But that didn't change her good opinion of me. She gave me "Wordly Wizard" workbooks, bunches of them, and she taught me words like *ointment* and *hypodermic*. See, she knew I wanted to be a nurse when I grew up. Me, Nurse Henderson, with a little white hat, all starched and pleated; white dress, white legs, white shoes, white shoelaces. Like an angel, only a little more starched and without the wings.

THREE

*T*HE CATFISH HOLLERED FROM DOWN PAST THE silver camper, the one that looked like a big toaster. He had a long, rolling laugh that he always topped off with a wild yelp of "Whoo-hoo mercy!"

Here comes nothing, I thought to myself. Of course I thought it to myself, how else could I think? You can't think to somebody else. Our brains are in our own skulls. So if you don't say it out loud, nobody hears it.

Mother's friend poured milk into my coffee. I looked down into my cup, watching the milk cloud swirling, knowing it would be the last quiet moment of the day. When the Catfish was on a tear, he kept everybody stirred up. His mood storms could get right scary. Not that he ever hit us; he didn't. If he ever hit my mother, it'd be the last thing those hands ever did—I'd see to that.

Pretty soon the Catfish came strolling up the path with his new friend, a short, swaggering guy with a chipped front tooth. Nobody was a stranger to the Catfish. He talked to people everywhere he went. Store clerks, traffic cops, even people in other cars sitting at stoplights.

"Angie, doll!" he called.

"I'm not your doll," the blond woman said flatly, and that did it for me. That Angie was a friend.

"Whatever." The Catfish brushed on. "I want you to meet an eligible bachelor. And I do mean eligible. This here's Gus Luna," he said, presenting his new friend with a sweeping gesture. "He's a self-made man, like me."

Gus smiled like he was so glad to be invited around the campfire with us. Hands down, Catfish was the king of the lonely people. (Don't tell anybody, but that's the one thing I liked about him.) And Catfish went to knee-slapping and howling "Whoo-hoo mercy!"

"Babe, sweetheart," he said—Babe was my mother's

name. Short for Barbara. "Did Angie bring enough coffee to offer a cup to my new best friend?"

Apparently, Angie was parked at the campsite next to
ours and was sharing her stuff with Mother, because, of
course, the Catfish had taken us camping with no equipment whatsoever.

Mother poured both men a cup of coffee. Catfish drank
his in a single gulp, wiped his mouth, and yowled, "Ruby
Clyde Henderson. I bet you ninety-to-nothing that you
think I forgot your special day." Then he and Gus put
their heads together and started to sing me "Happy
Birthday." I did not want to smile, having been dragged
halfway around the world without my permission, but I
couldn't help myself. Who could frown through their
own "Happy Birthday" song? The Catfish rushed over to
the car and got out the cake while he sang, "Happy birthday, dear— What the heck happened to your cake? Oh,
well, never mind, forget it."

He cut the cake with his pocketknife and put the pieces
right on our bare hands. While we ate, he went into the
car trunk and took out a big gift-wrapped box. "This is
part birthday present and part look-to-the-future present,

because I know it's hard for a kid to leave friends and whatnot. But one day you will thank me, Ruby Clyde. Remember this: A self-made man makes his own self."

I held the gift box in my lap. It was wrapped in pink and green teddy bears, with a huge gold ribbon, big as a cabbage. There was something so exciting about an unopened gift sitting and teasing me to tear the paper. But I never tore birthday wrapping, never.

Catfish was a big kid about my present, squirming and twisting like a puppy.

"Come on," he said.

"I will," I said.

"Sometime today, please," he said.

I ran my fingers around the edge of the box and began to loosen the tape.

"Oh, for crying out loud." He flapped his arms and said, "Just rip the stupid paper."

I threw the gold bow in the air, and he snatched at it like a dog with a ball. He tied the darn thing to his head and did the cha-cha for Mother. He could make her laugh, I'll give him that. That shiny bow kept the Catfish entertained while I enjoyed opening the rest of my present. I got the paper off without a single tear, then folded it flat to save.

I lifted the top off the box, and inside I found a real cowboy hat, real cowboy boots, a lasso, a holster with a toy gun, and rolls and rolls of caps. I was a little old for that getup, but I'm short with not much hair, and frankly, I loved that cowboy outfit. In fact, it may be about the best present I ever got.

But I saw Mother looking at my gun like it was a snake. "It's okay, Mother," I said, putting her hand on the plastic. "It's just a toy."

Catfish kept on blabbing. "Do you like it, girl? Do you? Does old Carl know how to pick 'em or what?"

I nodded, and as soon as he saw how much I really liked his present, he went on to something else. He was always in such a hurry, like he was swallowing food without chewing.

I put on my cowboy hat and tightened the thingy under my chin, then buckled the holster around my pajama waist and brushed dirt off my feet before stepping into the boots. I couldn't see myself, but I knew I was looking pretty good.

Angie, with her blond curls and crinkledy eyes, looked me up and down and said sincerely, "Suits you perfectly, kiddo."

Gus was telling us about his ex-wife and their divorce papers, and who got the car and who got the stereo. Mr. and Mrs. Gus thought they'd find something better if only they could get away from each other, but they never did, so they got back together but then broke up again.

Angie listened to him with her mouth half open, as if she couldn't believe that the Catfish was trying to match-make her with this guy. She told us that she was a recent widow, driving back to live with her family in Corpus Christi, so it was clear that she was not going to be dating Mr. Gus Luna. Angie was what I call "happy-sad": she smiled, but her flat blue eyes only made sunbursts of wrinkles from the corners of her eyelids.

Gus was telling us about working his way up from janitor to head cook at the Do-Nut Hole. He stopped and took a deep breath, then said, "Who'd have thunk it? Me, Gus Luna, would grow up to be the best doughnut cutter in Arkansas."

Catfish beamed like a lightbulb. "See what I told you? A self-made man, just like me."

So we're in Arkansas, I thought. Arkansas was a long way from home. I was loading my new cap gun and trying to call up a picture of the U.S. map in my head. I aimed my pistol and shot the coffeepot. *Crack!* It went way louder than just the cap gun because at the same time the log popped hot sap. Mother jumped out of her skin, which sent the old Catfish into great peals of laughter and knee-slapping and that "Whoo-hoo mercy!" that he so enjoyed. But it wasn't funny, I hadn't meant to frighten her, so I put the gun away and held her hand.

"Everything's okay. Who knew a little toy would make such a noise?" I rubbed my thumb across the top of her hand until she quit her shivers.

Mother didn't like guns, you know, what with my father getting killed and all.

·············●●·············

I BETTER TELL THAT STORY NOW. HERE, I'LL TELL IT fast. It's a bad story, so get ready. See, my mother was pregnant with me, and she was married to my father, who was a *prince of a guy*. She always called him a *real prince of a guy*. And everything was beautiful for them until one day they went to the lake for a picnic, and right there on a bright sunny day, eating chocolate brownies with pecans, they were robbed. And the robber, who was just a jumpy kid, my mother said, shot and killed my father. He took the wallet from my father's hand, and instead of just running away, he shot my father.

I keep wondering about that shot. A tiny bit of time, a single action that ripped up lives forever and can never be undone. Why on earth did he shoot my father? And why did he *not* shoot my mother—and me inside of her? I can understand why he might steal wallets—a person can really need money—but what possible good comes from shooting a man? I'll never ever know his answer to that, because they never caught him. He's probably walking around like a normal person and nobody knows he's a murderer. Not only was he a murderer, but he stole part of my life, taking away my father and leaving me with the likes of the Catfish.

But that horrible day at the lake, Mother was so shocked by the violence and loss that I started to get born. I think I was trying to take care of her even then. Between the policemen and the ambulances, she just barely made it to the hospital. I was a preemie in an incubator with lung things, and heart things, and needle things; and six weeks later she took me home in a shoe box. And that was about all she could take of this runaround world.

That's also why Mother has a little problem celebrating my birthday. It was not a festive day. And birthdays are, by definition, festive. Why, it was six years before I could even get her to tell the day I was born. "Which one you want to know?" she said. "The day you were born, the day you were supposed to be born, or the day you came home from the hospital? 'Cause they were all pretty far apart."

It sounds like Mother was a careless woman, but she was not. She's everything I wanted in a mom. Sometimes she would just give me my own day, out of the blue. "This is *your* day, Ruby Clyde," she'd say. But never on my birthday. I wouldn't celebrate that day either, not if I were her. What she'd been through! And she's never once acted like it was my fault.

FOUR

*T*HE CATFISH WAS IN A HURRY TO LEAVE THE campground, of course. Gus and he were going into town to do some business, *manly bidness*, he said, like he was president of the United States or something. Last time the Catfish did some business, we ended up with a hundred hamster cages in the living room. Don't ask. Catfish was a *businessman*, you know. He slipped behind the steering wheel, gunned the engine, and yowled, "Get in."

Mother and I looked at each other.

Angie stood and leaned over the fire. "Go on, I will wash my coffeepot."

"Why can't we stay here?" I asked, because I wanted nothing to do with the Catfish's business, whatever it was. Nothing good ever came from his big ideas.

"I'd be glad to have the company," Angie offered. I looked at her yellow car and wondered if she might just drive us all the way back home. We'd wait for the Catfish to go to town with Gus Luna, then skedaddle.

But he was having none of that. The Catfish flailed around—"Oh shoot, just get in the car because I ain't driving all the way back out here to get you. Gus has a friend I need to meet. When me and Gus finish our bidness we are leaving Arkansas and heading to Texaw. Get it? Get it?"

And as much as I liked wordplay I wasn't about to give him the benefit of the laugh. It only made me dizzy that I was going to have to listen to Catfish say Texaw for however long it took to drive across the biggest state in the union, except for Alaska, which doesn't count because it's not connected—all ice, no roads, just oil rigs and polar bears. And who in their right mind would want to drive across Alaska anyway?

Mother did what he said. She got in the backseat.

I wanted, more than anything else on earth, for Mother to get out of that car and stay at the campsite with Angie. Then take me back home where we belonged. But she didn't. Instead she patted the seat, asking me to get in and sit beside her. I did, reluctantly. As we drove away, Angie stood with the coffeepot in one hand and waved. The morning sun caught her blond curls and formed a halo around her head. If only she were an angel, she could . . . well, it was too late.

Mother held my hand, absentmindedly tickling my palm with her pinky. We sped out of the campground, which I did not like one little bit, because the campground was full of dogs and children and it would have been just like the reckless Catfish to run over some of them.

We had left so fast that I was still wearing my pajamas, so I had to change in the car. Mother held a blanket to shield me from the men while I undressed. I dug my jeans out of the tangled wad of clothes they stuffed in bags for me—all the while thinking the whole day, my whole life (except for my new cowboy accessories), was a mess, and I had no entire clue how to fix it.

I talked from behind the blanket. "What the heck are we supposed to do while you and Gus conduct your business?"

"Why, sightsee, of course," Catfish said.

"Sightsee?" I said. I had never been sightseeing in my life. Never even thought about it. I wasn't even sure what it was, except maybe looking at Niagara Falls or the Grand Canyon, things from picture books. "You mean like going to see the Statue of Liberty?"

"Ruby Clyde," Catfish said, "sometimes I think you are as dumb as a box of rocks."

Imagine somebody like the Catfish calling you dumb. I yanked on my new boots, trying not to like my cowboy outfit after his crack about my intelligence. I didn't want to be beholden to the Catfish, but I couldn't help myself; I just loved my boots and hat, lasso and gun. Once I had them all back on, Mother dropped the blanket.

I leaned over the seat between the men and listened to them do man-talk.

"Hot Springs is just hopping with sights to see," Gus the Doughnut Cutter bragged, since he was the local expert. He went on about these Duck Trucks and the IQ

Zoo, which was full of smart animals—something I definitely needed to see. Better than Niagara Falls, the Grand Canyon, and the Statue of Liberty all rolled into one.

I asked if there were any hot springs in Hot Springs.

"Oh lordy, yes," Gus said. "Everywhere. That's why they call it Hot Springs, silly." He told us the hot springs water was supposed to heal the sick. I liked the sound of healing waters, what with my interest in nursing. He said the water trickles down to the center of the earth, gets boiling hot, and shoots back up. Takes about two thousand years to go down and only about a minute to come back up.

"Whoo-hoo mercy!" said Catfish. "Would you listen to Professor Gus, I'd a never taken you for a schooly man."

"Shut your face, Carl," Gus said.

"Who's going to make me?" Catfish said.

Gus clenched a little fist and showed his teeth. Catfish made a fist too and they boxed at each other until a wheel caught the edge of the road and hit gravel. Gus cried, "Watch the darn road, why don't you?"

"You watch it," Catfish said.

"No, you," Gus said. And that went on for a while. They really liked each other, that much was clear.

Catfish turned the steering wheel and said, "I got a friend in Hollywood. The one we're going to see. He's a real big shot to the stars."

"I know exactly what you mean," Gus said. "It reminds me of my extra good friend in Austin. He's a big shot to the music people. That's the place to be. They just throw money at you in Austin."

"Oh yeah?" Catfish said. "How good a friend?"

"Bosom buddies," said Gus.

"I don't believe you for a minute," Catfish said.

"True," said Gus, "go there and call him. Tell him Gus Luna sent you. He used to be a doughnut cutter with me, but now he's rolling in the dough."

The Catfish swerved the car off the side of the road just to make his new friend shut up.

⋯⋯••••●•••••••⋯

.

CATFISH LET US OUT ON THE STREET CORNER NONE TOO soon, and he put a hundred-dollar bill in Mother's hand.

"Don't ever say Carl doesn't take care of his women," he said, showing off for Gus the Doughnut Cutter. Mother put the money in her purse. You might think Catfish was rich because he had hundred-dollar bills and all, but he wasn't. It was just that he was a construction worker on houses and offices and things and they paid him in cash. That's what Mother told me. Maybe he stole it. Who knew?

Before he left, we agreed to meet back up at the big fountain at some certain time in the afternoon. "Exact o'clock!" Catfish said. "And don't be late or I'll ditch you." He shouldn't have said that—it frightened Mother. But I couldn't have been happier with the thought of him leaving us. I could get Mother back home where we belonged, no trouble. Come to think of it, if he was going to leave us there in Hot Springs, Arkansas, he should have just left us at home to begin with.

FIVE

FTER CATFISH LEFT US ON THE CORNER, Mother and I decided to drink water from a hot spring, ride a Duck, and visit the IQ Zoo—in that order. Saved the best for last, and that worked good, because the IQ Zoo was where I met Bunny the Pig.

We found our first sight and saw it—a real hot spring. Sure enough, that old water was hot. We even drank it.

I thought about the water sloshing around in my stomach. And my stomach wasn't the final destination. That two-thousand-year-old water would come out of my body one way or the other, and make its way back down to the center of the earth to be shot up to some space visitors in two thousand years. I'd be dead and gone. Everybody I knew would be long gone. The circle of life gave me the willies.

I took Mother's hand firmly. The sidewalk was busy with people coming and going, in and out of the big fancy hotels. I was proud to be strutting there in my new cowboy outfit. We fell in behind a couple of big girls who walked with great confidence on platform shoes. They wore long skirts made of bright handkerchiefs stitched together, and their tops didn't all the way cover their backs so I could see their knobby spines swaying like cobras. I didn't think I would ever be that beautiful when I grew up, if I agreed to let myself grow up. I might just be a Peter Pan. Who wants to be a stupid old adult?

••••••••••●••••••••••

SIGHT TWO: THE DUCK TRUCKS. THEY WERE ADVERTISED everywhere. We paid to take a ride. I used Mother's hundred-dollar bill, with a picture of Ben Franklin on it. For change I got a fifty-dollar bill, with Ulysses S. Grant on it. I'd never seen a fifty-dollar bill before. Also got a twenty, and a five, plus coins. As I said, I could handle money. Before she died, my mean grandmother told me all about counting the change because people would keep more, hoping you wouldn't notice. "Sneaky snakes" she called them. Her world was full of sneaky snakes and, more often than not, she made me feel like a sneaky snake.

The Hot Springs Duck did not have feathers. It was part tank, part houseboat, and part open-air bus—if you can mix those three. When all the seats on the Duck Truck were filled, the tour guides jumped on the platform by the driver and grabbed the microphones. They were a couple of old people in overalls and big straw hats. Grannie rocked back and yelled, "Howdeeeee."

I "howdeed" back at them. All the adults smiled kindly at me, but all the kids looked at me like I was some kind of maniac. I didn't care, not a titch. It doesn't cost you anything to be polite.

Then the Duck sped down a boat ramp and paddled out into the lake with a great splash. Everybody on the Duck screamed, myself included. We all knew it was coming, that big splashdown, but we all screamed just the same. It's funny what groups of people will do just to be part of a group. Scream, laugh, riot, fall on your knees and pray.

As we picked up steam and paddled away from land, I took Mother's hand in mine. "Let's go home," I said.

"I don't know, sweetie." She loosened her fingers.

"I do, Mom. We probably have enough money to get a bus or a plane or a taxi."

"That would be dangerous." Mother pulled her hand away and ran it over her forehead, brushing windblown hair back.

"Not as dangerous as being with Carl and Gus the Doughnut Cutter. They're up to no good, I tell you."

"Don't be silly, Ruby Clyde."

As I said, Mother was a good mother, no joke. It's just that she was so busy avoiding danger that she never saw it right under her nose. As my mean grandmother used to say, "If it had been a snake, I'd'a bit it."

When we got across the lake, a baby in a lime-green sunhat went to screaming. The mother kept shoving a pacifier in its mouth but she couldn't hush it up for nothing, and there we were, stuck out on the water. People started rolling their eyes and looking as miserable as the screaming baby.

Finally Mother leaned over to me and whispered, "Ruby Clyde, could you do something?" Mother liked my healing powers, even though they were limited, at that time, to crying. She believed in me.

I shook my head. "Not in front of all these people."

She nudged my arm and said, "Go on, put your hands on that poor child."

Mother nagged me like the mother of Jesus at Cana, when she wanted him to turn the water into wine. Now if that wasn't a trite miracle, nothing was. I mean, what possible difference could it make if the wedding guests had to drink water instead of wine? Grandmother said water was poisoned back then and wine was healthier (but that was no excuse to drink it today, she said). I don't think the mother of Jesus was worried about their health anyway—she just wanted wine.

Finally, I said, "*Oh* all right." Then I stood up and walked toward the crying baby. The baby screamed louder, its face all rubbery with fury. The mother seemed scared of me when I stopped in front of them, but before she could interfere I laid my hand on the baby's little green hat. The baby made a perfect O with its mouth and blinked. Tears caught in its eyelashes, and it got quiet—completely quiet. I took my hand away and said to the mother, "There."

Everyone on the Duck stared at me.

·············●·············

THE NEXT SIGHT: THE IQ ZOO. THE BIG WINDOWS WERE painted black with big yellow words: IQ ZOO. The wall had cartoon elephants, camels, cobras, and ostriches, all holding college diplomas and those flat-top hats that people wear to graduation.

What a wondrous variety of animals. My hopes escalated, and I almost forgot that I had been dragged away from home without my permission on my birthday. In addition to the animal pictures, there were circus people painted on the windows. I'd always thought it would be quite nice to join the circus.

A miserable teenager was selling tickets at the IQ Zoo. He rocked back on a stool, smoking a cigarette and looking pained beyond his years. It was the circus outfit he was wearing that made him look so put out. He was hawking the business with a little jingle: "Come see the IQ Zoo, say who? You is who should come see the IQ Zoo, say who? You's who should . . ." Something about that boy gave me the willies.

It cost twenty-six dollars for the two of us to go inside. I hated to let it go, but I paid with that fancy fifty-dollar bill. The unhappy boy took old Ulysses S. Grant, then counted back change: one, two, three, four single-dollar bills, and then he stopped and looked over my shoulder at the next customer, like maybe I wouldn't notice that he was stealing my money. I stayed put and squinted hard at him until he slid the twenty across the counter. He was a sneaky snake, if ever I saw one.

Inside the showroom, a big round man wore red-striped circus pants, gathered at the ankles. A shapely woman and a little girl wore red majorette costumes with black top hats and batons. I was pretty sure it was a family business. I mean, I don't think that little girl would be there without her parents. There's such a thing as child labor laws.

The Circus Dad sang into a microphone while a bunch of chickens performed a square dance. Yes sir, they did. *Promenade and do-si-do your partner!* If you don't believe it, go to the IQ Zoo and see for yourself. You will find square-dancing chickens with little red kerchiefs tied around their necks. The people cheered for those chickens and the chickens seemed right proud of themselves.

Mother was not amused. She had a soft spot for animals. I did too, but hers was bigger and softer.

After the chicken dance came Noah's Ark. The spotlight swiveled to a big boat, like a Duck Truck, on a shallow pond of water. There was a wide ramp attached. Out of the dark came the voice of God:

"Make thee an ark of gopher wood . . ."

And while I was pondering a tree made of critters, the Circus Mom and Circus Girl pranced around in their matching majorette costumes and began herding the animals up the ramp onto the ark. They poked the poor animals with silver batons.

You know the rest. So there they came: white mice, hamsters, chickens, ducks, dogs, cats, and green parakeets—two by two. I was deeply disappointed. That seemed like a puny boat full of punier animals, what with the outside window promising camels and snakes and ostriches. Those were just a bunch of house pets. Where were the exotics we had paid to see?

The lights dimmed and Circus God said his business about raining for forty days and forty nights. While he talked, Circus Mom rocked the boat. The little Circus Girl brought out a sprinkler and sprayed rain. Oh, those animals looked miserable indeed, and I wondered how many times a day they had to suffer the ultimate wrath of God.

So anyway, the storm got over. The lights came up while the animals shook water off their feathers and fur. At this point a lovely white dove flew down from the darkness, and with a sweep of his wings, he landed on a perch atop the ark. The bird held an olive branch in his mouth, or some kind of twig that was supposed to be an olive branch. And that was that.

The room went black. Suddenly a rainbow flashed on the far wall and God recited from the darkness: *"I do set my bow in the cloud and it shall be a token of a covenant between me and this earth, between me and you and every living creature of all flesh."*

My mother didn't like Noah's Ark, not one little bit. She said out loud, "I hope you plan to wipe those animals dry. They're going to catch their death." Circus God snapped his head around and bugged his eyes at my mother. I, myself, was surprised at her boldness, but before I could give it much thought, it was time for the next animal show.

A spot lit up the center ring and—Lord help me—they had a little pink pig driving a miniature Cadillac. Around and around he went, American flags waving off the back of the little gold car. Everyone laughed except my mother, who raised her voice. "Now *this* is carrying things too far. A pig is an intelligent animal."

Circus God spun around and said, "Excuse me," like he was the polite one, which he was not, in case you hadn't noticed. What he was really saying to her was *shut up*.

"You are not excused," Mother said right back. I had never heard her speak that way to anybody on earth, but as I said before, she was right queer about animals, especially intelligent ones such as you might expect to find in the IQ Zoo. People around us began to squirm. The little pig drove around and around, honking his horn. That was not sightseeing at its finest.

Mother raised her fingers up and rubbed her forehead like she was suffering a splitting headache. Then she whispered to me, "Pay attention. I have to break that pig out of here."

Before I could understand that Mother was suggesting stealing the pig, Circus Girl jumped forward, her majorette uniform sparkling all over. She pointed at us and screamed, "Daddy, Daddy, that boy and his mother are going to steal our pig!"

I guess, to her, everybody who doesn't wear a majorette uniform is a boy.

When I turned back around, Mother had already rushed into the ring and was pulling the pig from the Cadillac. "Let him free!" she cried.

Well, the entire firmament of a red-striped family was on us. Circus God jumped on Mother and dragged her toward the door. That's when the gloomy teenager who took our money at the entrance threw me over his shoulder, my cowboy boots cycling uselessly in the air. I hated feeling helpless, but that seemed to be a byproduct of being smaller than everybody else; that's why small people have to use their brains.

Mother's shoe flew off when she was tossed out. Landing outside on our behinds was humiliating, but what could we do? Who heard complaints from the poor in spirit and poor in money? Nobody, that's who. Especially when it was just plain legal cruelty and bad manners.

Mother stood up off the sidewalk, smoothed her hair, and brushed the dirt off her skirt. As she straightened her shoe back onto her foot she said, "Ruby Clyde, they may own that pig legally, but not rightfully. Some things are just plain wrong."

SIX

*B*Y THE TIME WE GOT BACK TO THE MEETING place at the water fountain, Catfish was jumping out of his skin. "Well, take your pretty time, ladies! Don't mind old Carl. He's just the chauffeur. He don't matter. Carl's got nothing better to do than wait all day on a couple of sightseers."

He hadn't waited *all day*, but I bit my tongue. We jumped into the car and he drove away. What happened next defies explanation.

"Where's the doughnut head?" I asked, seeing his new best friend was gone. But he didn't answer.

Catfish reached between his legs under the seat and

pulled out a big gray pistol. A real metal one. He was driving with one hand and waving that gun around with the other. I was quite speechless. Did he not respect my mother's history? I turned to Mother, expecting her to be falling apart, but she hadn't seen the gun. She was staring out the car window at billboards, gone off in that world of hers.

I looked back at the gun. First real one I had ever been close to, not counting the one that killed my father when I was inside my mother. I couldn't have seen that one, but I bet I felt it through my mother's blood, because you know it laid her out so it must have laid me out too. What kind of memory would that be?

The Catfish's gun did not look like my showy little cap gun. It was more boring and more real. Long and plain and heavy looking. I was hypnotized. I mean, one pull of that trigger right there under his finger and people could die—forever. And that was a sobering thought, indeed. How could a little piece of metal force itself into your body and displace enough body parts to kill you dead? I have noticed, by the way, that death is often caused by two things trying to be in the same place at the same time, like two cars on the same stretch of highway, or a bullet and a heart. Because of this insight, I am not convinced that world peace is possible, what with everything fighting over limited space.

Mother finally saw the gun and screamed.

Catfish drove up on the sidewalk. "Woman!" he yelled.

I banged the Catfish on the shoulder and screamed, "Use your brain! Get that gun out of her face."

Catfish stomped the brakes. "Holy crow! What did I ever do to deserve such a woman?" (I'd been asking myself that same question ever since he showed up in our lives.)

The car skidded to a stop. Mother gathered herself together, straightened her skirt, and sniffed proudly, "I've had a very difficult day, Carl, and it is just too much for me to see a gun. You know, I do not approve of guns."

"And guns don't approve of you, Babe."

I wished somebody would just take out his voice box. The whole world would be better if the Catfish opened his big mouth and said absolutely nothing.

But Mother didn't scream at him or anything. She was very quiet. Long pause.

I was waiting for her to say something, like maybe she would say, *Shut up, Carl, we're going home whether you like it or not.* She could have said that, but she didn't.

What she said was, "I would like very much for you to use your new gun to get me a pig."

The Catfish's jaw fell open.

Mine too.

And she told him about the IQ Zoo. As far-fetched as she sounded, I liked her idea of saving that pig. My only regret to having been kicked out, literally, of the IQ Zoo was that we had left without the pig.

Somebody had to entice the Catfish to get that pig, and again, that somebody was me. It was a good thing I understood him. Nothing worked better with the Catfish than to call his manhood into question. So I said, "Wait a minute, what was all that talk about using that gun to protect her from bullies?"

"Whatchoo talkin' 'bout? What bullies?"

"Bullies," I said, "violent bullies." So I told him about getting shoved out of the IQ Zoo so hard that Mother fell down and lost her shoe.

"Babe, is that true?" He turned those wide-spaced eyes on Mother.

She nodded.

He looked at her for two or three long seconds, and I swear I could see his temperature rise. Just like in the cartoons.

Suddenly he hit the accelerator and did a U-turn right over the median, heading for the IQ Zoo. He ran red lights and yield signs and skidded to a stop across the street from the place.

"Don't move," he said, kicking the car door open.

The next moments stretched in time like elastic, then snapped back with the sound of gunfire. I knew it when I heard it. Strange, since I had never heard a real gunshot before. Dull loud pops came from inside the building. Gunshots. My throat was full of cement.

Before I could catch a lungful of air, the Catfish came flying out the door. That little pig was under his arm like a football. He pointed his pistol at the sky and fired again while he ran, bony knees popping up real high with each step. A gang of crazies chased him out: Circus God in his bright baggies; the son in his unhappiness; then the mother and daughter in their majorette uniforms; angry men too, from the audience, shouting and shaking their fists.

And there came the Catfish, happier than I had ever seen him.

He tossed the pig over the seat to me and jumped behind the wheel. "Whoo-hoo mercy!" he hollered as the car fishtailed and sprayed gravel all over the mob.

The piglet in my arms was about as cuddly as a bag of potatoes. He went to squealing and crawling up my neck, stabbing me with those hard, pointy feet. That little guy was so excited, I decided to lay my healing hands on him. And it was the quickest healing I have ever done. Just like that, the piglet flopped across my lap and fell asleep.

I stroked that strange hairy skin of my beautiful new pig and felt a tiny bit of softness toward the Catfish, who had rescued him. The piglet was an even better birthday present than the cowboy outfit, but the gift-giver was a big fat mess. The Catfish could have given me a gift every day for the rest of my life and it wouldn't have made him the kind of adult who should have been with my mother, not a man who could replace my prince of a father.

SEVEN

WE DROVE OUT OF HOT SPRINGS STRAIGHT into the afternoon sun. "Sunset Boulevard— Here! We! Come!" The Catfish'd slap the steering wheel and laugh, then say it again a few miles down the road. Mother glanced over her shoulder at the sleeping pig and smiled at me. After a while we rode in peaceful silence. Then Mother's head leaned to one side and she slept. She needed her sleep, I knew. It had been a long day for both of us, but I didn't like her going to sleep and leaving me alone with the Catfish.

Right on cue, at her first soft snore, the Catfish cut his eyes up in the rearview mirror. Those eyes, those floating eyes, gave me the willies. "What you going to call that pig?" he said.

I looked down at the pig's upturned snout, little round nostrils like hole punches.

"Bunny," I said. That was the name of my best friend back home, and I missed her so much it hurt my teeth, especially since she would be looking for me on my birthday. I worried who would tell her what had become of me.

"Bunny!" Catfish complained. "That's a stupid name for a boy pig—a famous car-driving pig! Call him Dale Earnhardt."

I held firm. "He's a Bunny," I said, thinking, *So what if it's a girl-boy name*. I could be a Ruby or a Clyde whenever I wanted. If nothing else, I believed a pig named Bunny would keep me from being homesick. Suddenly my stomach filled with rocks. I wanted to go home. I'd even be glad to see Mr. Upchuck, the eyeless wonder.

The Catfish muttered and turned on the radio, changed stations a hundred times, then switched it off. A piece of sunlight cut across my mother's hair.

"Carl," I said. I never called him Catfish to his face.

"Yu-huh?" He raised his eyes into the rearview mirror again.

"When are we going back home?"

"Not till I've got something to show for it."

"There's nothing for us in Hollywood."

"Well, aren't you the smarty-pants Queen of the World?"

"I just want to be home and go to my own school. I'm missing the end-of-school party."

"School shmool. Who needs school? I never learned nuthin' in school."

Well, that was obvious, but I didn't say so. I folded the piglet's ear between my fingers.

We whizzed past a tall skinny guy standing on the side of the road. His curly hair pyramided out to his shoulders. He had a guitar hung over one shoulder and held a hand-painted sign saying NEW MEXICO.

"What's that guy doing?" I asked.

"That is a hitchhiker. He wants somebody to give him a ride where he's going."

"A stranger's going to pick him up?"

"What do you think, Ruby Clyde? You think he knows everybody driving along this road?"

"But people do that? Stop and pick him up and drive him where he's going?"

"Sure, people hitchhike all the time, but they don't always take you where you are going. They just take you as far as they're going, then they boot you out and you have to catch another ride."

That was good news: I could hitchhike home.

"So put me out, Carl. I'll hitchhike." I'd get out on the road like that New Mexico person, only my sign would say HOME.

"I should do that." He laughed. "I should do that while your mother is still asleep."

"Okay," I lifted my chin. "Just pull over, anywhere along the shoulder is fine."

"You can't do that, Ruby Clyde. Where would you live? What would you eat?"

"Somewhere, something," I said.

"How about money, where you going to get that?"

"Same place everybody else does—I'll get a job."

"A job! That's a laugh. You think jobs are just out there waiting to be had?"

"No, it's not a laugh. I could be a nurse." I straightened Bunny's tail, then let it curl around my finger.

"A nurse! Whoo-hoo mercy!"

"I could too be a nurse, everybody says so. I help out all the time in the school infirmary."

"You're not at the school infirmary anymore."

I don't know why I wasted my breath on the Catfish. He was too stupid to be a nurse, but I wasn't. Sometimes he just went out of his way to make me feel bad about myself.

He kept on, saying things he wouldn't say if Mother were awake. "Do you know what happens to children without adults? Do you? If they're not killed and eaten by maniacs, the police pick them up and put them in an orphanage."

"What!"

"Yes, an orphanage."

"What if I don't want to go to an orphanage?"

"Too bad. You don't get a vote. They lock you in an orphanage until you're eighteen years old. Haven't you ever read *Oliver Copperfield*? He was an orphan who grew up to be a magician, but not before he got taught a lot of tricks by this cool dude, Fagin."

"That's stupid," I said, and quit talking. He got the title wrong, and the story. I'd read *Oliver Twist* at school.

Okay, it was only the short version; it's called abridged when they make a long story short, like chopping out parts and building a bridge so you still get the main story. He was right about Oliver being an orphan. I tried not to believe the Catfish, about me being put in an orphanage, but I couldn't help it, the damage was done. *Holy moly*. I was going to be thinking about getting caught and being put in an orphanage for the rest of my life. Stupid Catfish. Why did he put that in my brain? Talk about the unearned willies.

Catfish drove up on the tail of a big hauling truck. That truck was chock-full of cows, just like children in an orphanage. I could see bony tails swatting at their hind legs. Big wobbly eyes stared at me through the slats. Ears rotated on their heads. Poor orphan cows smashed into the dark truck.

When we got past the cow truck, we sped up.

There was nothing to do but block the Catfish out of my mind, all his talk about orphanages—I was stuck in the car, but my brain could go anywhere.

I pulled out my workbooks. Some hangman puzzles fell out; my friend Bunny and I used to play those. I had stumped her with P_IG_T. The word was *plight*. She guessed six times—got a head, body, arm, arm, leg, and leg and then hung. *Plight* was a good word; people forget about the G-H-T. I flipped the pages, visiting words like old friends. *Porcine, piggish, hoggish.* (Just a vocabulary word last year, now I was a Pig Owner, myself.) *Perturb, irksome*—two of my favorite words. When my mean grandmother would use them to describe me I'd shout out "Wordly Wizard" like the teacher taught us to do when we heard one of our words out in the world. That always confused my grandmother just before it made her mad. She liked everything to be orderly and biblical— her version only. She's the reason I have the whole book memorized, practically, at least the parts she liked, with the definitions she liked. Once I read the real definition of *faith* to her: the firm belief in something for which there is no tangible proof. "Blasphemy," she cried. "What are you doing reading books by wizards?"

The wind was whistling all around the car. Along comes this monster pickup truck, it pulled up alongside us, and I saw that New Mexico hitchhiker sitting in the flatbed holding his hair like it might blow away. I pressed up against my window and waved; he waved back. I pulled Bunny up and waved his little hoof and New Mexico laughed. The pickup driver took off like a rocket, blasting past us, like he owned the world. It's weird all the people you see in this world that you will never see again. All those cars, sidewalks, buildings just full of people and you go right past them, then you never ever see them again. What is the point of so many people everywhere?

As the truck pulled away I wished New Mexico would be my friend and take me home. I didn't even care if I had to sit outside like that.

···········•●•···········

EIGHT

···········•●•···········

OTHER WOKE UP, FINALLY, AND THAT FREED me from the stinky Catfish, who'd scared me silly with all that talk about the orphanage. I couldn't take it anymore; if I was going to be stuck in the car all night, I wanted Mother awake. One of her lovely arms stretched straight up. She put a flattened palm on the ceiling of the car and pressed. "Yow—ohhhhh," she yawned, then sighed and looked around. "Where are we?"

"Somewhere," Catfish answered.

"Anybody hungry?" she asked.

We mentioned my birthday cake and the box of doughnuts. "Bleh!" Mother said, and reached for a doughnut.

While I daydreamed about hitchhiking home, Mother pinched off bites of her doughnut and offered them to Bunny. The little pig nibbled the sweet off her fingers. It's funny how dainty pigs can be. And polite too. When Bunny chewed his sugar doughnut, he blinked his little round eyes at me and smiled.

We settled in for a long stretch of driving. The green trees gave way to dry rock and the sunset turned the sky blood orange. That was the first full day I had ever spent driving in a car, and it is odd, being on top of each other like that for so long. You *talk and talk and talk*, then you stop talking and *think and think and think*. After a while you go back to talking.

To pass the time I reached forward and brushed Mother's hair. There was nothing quite like the smell of my mother's hair. It was floral but human—like what babies would smell like if they came out of the earth on stalks, wrapped in fresh spring leaves. I brushed all of her hair, from the scalp down to the tips. She enjoyed it so much she purred.

"Carl!" Suddenly Mother leaned forward and read a road sign. "Is this the right road?"

"I'm always on the right road," he said, as if that were the stone-cold truth.

"But . . ." Mother wanted to agree with him but she knew something was wrong.

He interrupted her and said, "This is the absolutely correcto road because I am taking a detour to Austin."

Mother slammed back against the seat and raised both hands to her face.

"What's wrong with you, Babe? Gus Luna said Austin is a great place to make a little money. Besides which, you have that sister there. Can't we invite ourselves to stay?"

What was he blabbing about? Mother didn't have a sister. I gathered her hair into a thick ponytail, trying to brush it again. Mother kept silent.

"Earth to Babe," Catfish said, never one to be sensitive. "You going to answer me, or what?"

Mother said carefully, "Yes, Carl. I have a sister near Austin. A little town in the Hill Country, called Cypress Mill."

That was news to me; Mother had a sister. *News* isn't a big enough word. It was a bomb in my skull.

Mother lowered her voice, making it harder for me to hear her. I stretched my eardrums, trying to learn more about Mother's secret. When she said the words *I have a sister* it sounded like she was out of her mind, like she was saying *I have a Martian.*

"What's her name?" Catfish asked.

"Eleanor," she whispered.

"Eleanor Henderson?" Catfish asked.

"No, Carl. Henderson is my married name, not hers. She is Eleanor Rose."

"Rose! Is that your maiden name? Bed of Roses." Catfish laughed at himself because nobody else ever did.

"Hardly." Mother reached one hand back and pulled her hair out of my hands. She brought it in front of her shoulder where I couldn't reach it. "Excuse me, Carl. Why are we talking about my sister?"

"I *told* you once already, we're driving right through Austin. Be a free place to stay. Don't you want a free place to stay?"

"Not really," Mother said. "And she probably wouldn't have me."

"Aww, come on, Babe, she's your own flesh and blood."

"She's more than that," Mother said. "She's my twin."

I dropped the brush. Sister was one thing; twin was another. I tried hard to remember if my mean grandmother had ever hinted at this, or if she had kept photographs in the house, or anything to remind her of her daughter. Nothing.

Twins, I kept thinking and suddenly I asked, "Identical?" I'd seen identical twins in movies, and who doesn't daydream about having a long-lost identical twin? Ruby Clyde One and Ruby Clyde Two.

"Why yes, identical," Mother said, as if she had forgotten.

Identical! I sat back hard, bouncing my head against the seat. Imagine that. Another person on this earth who looked exactly like my mother.

"You never told me any of this," I said, wondering what all else she hadn't told me.

Mother pursed her lips, then rolled her eyes and said, "Well, she didn't wish to have me in her life. Besides, she's a nun."

"You Catholic?!" the Catfish yelled.

"No," I said, but they both ignored me. My mean

grandmother didn't trust Catholics, I never knew why, but we weren't Catholics, that much was sure. Grandmother's church argued about everything and splintered about ten times, always moving down the road to be the new church of something—adding words like *truth*, *light*, and *holy*—all good words, but they seemed tacked on and wrong.

Mother watched the last bit of sun drop below the horizon with an orange pop. She sighed and said, "I'm not much of anything, churchwise. Eleanor is Episcopalian. They're a pretty loosey-goosey, do-whatever-you-want kind of church."

I'd never heard the word *Episcopalian* and didn't even care to look it up I was so flummoxed by having a mystery aunt. (To tell the truth, I did look it up later. See, Henry VIII had to get out of the Catholic Church so he could divorce one wife and cut off the head of another. He called his church Anglican, which means Church of England, and it couldn't have been much of a church if you ask me. Episcopal is the American version of that church; they allow divorce but not beheadings and they aren't really bad at all.)

"Oh well," huffed Catfish and stuck his nose up in the

air. "Never mind. Old Carl's got nun use for a nun, want nun of that, nun-thing worse than a nun. Whoo-hoo mercy! Thanks a *lot*, Babe. As usual, good old Carl will have to come up with a better plan."

"Honestly, Carl. Enough, already," Mother said.

An identical twin and a nun! My mind was spinning with the image: a person who looked just like my mother, dressed like a nun. A nun. They looked like witches to me.

My hand wandered down and stroked the little pig, which was asleep on the seat beside me. He squirmed a bit, opened his little eyes, and looked up at me, like I was his mother. Then he rolled back into sleep with a twitch of his nose.

······●······

WE RODE FOR THE LONGEST TIME IN SILENCE, WHICH was so very unusual for the Catfish. But it happened. We had more driving to do and I hoped we weren't all talked out, because I certainly wanted to hear more about Eleanor Rose.

Finally, out of nowhere, Mother began to speak with a soft, storytelling tone in her voice. There is something about being surrounded by night that makes everybody want to tell scary stories or secrets. Mother's story was both.

"We were like night and day. Eleanor was always angry, fighting with our mother. I'd do anything to keep Mother happy. I don't know why we were different that way. Then Eleanor got herself pregnant. She went away to a secret place to give the baby up for adoption. It broke her heart."

Mother kept on, "So when I got pregnant with Ruby and decided to marry Walter, Eleanor went into a dark place. She left town and never looked back. I called her when Ruby Clyde was about three, hoping she had softened, but she said she never wanted to see me or my child. It hurt me, but giving that baby up for adoption had blackened her life. Before she left, Eleanor said not a day passed she didn't wonder where that boy-child was, and if he had gotten into a good home or a bad one. It left a black hole in her heart. Since Walter died, I understand having a black hole in your heart, and if I were to ever lose Ruby Clyde, well, there would not be blackness enough."

She took a deep breath and so did I. What would you

do if there wasn't enough blackness in the world to describe your feelings? Invent a new color? Not that blackness is a color, I knew that. Blackness is black. It didn't matter anyway because Mother was never going to lose me, not while I was alive.

The tires hit the highway cracks in a regular rhythm. We listened to the road song until Catfish said, "So, okay, as I said before—we won't look up the nun."

Mother hadn't told him the half of it. My grandmother was harsh times a hundred. She took my mother in after my father was killed. Raised me with a Bible in one hand and a stick in the other. I'm not saying I hated her, I'm just saying I spent half my life under our bed. Grandmother taught me how to get by in the real world. Mean people have an edge and it's good to learn their techniques. She's the reason I could take care of my mother as well as I did. I was nine, almost ten, when Grandmother died and I'd taken care of us ever since—that is until the Catfish came along and messed everything up.

I wanted to find her, Eleanor Rose, the nun who lived in Cypress Mill, and not for a free place to stay, like what the Catfish wanted, although I did have a selfish motive.

I thought maybe she could talk some sense into my mother, help us get back home. Also I was more than a little curious about seeing her—her being identical to my mother and all. It didn't seem possible, no matter how hard I tried, to imagine another person looking exactly like my mother. But they were *strange* from each other, and they seemed to like it like that.

One thing was clear though: I had been the cause of their strangeness, and that made me a burden and probably not the one to get them to be friends again. What a rotten pregnancy Mother had with me—lost her sister at the beginning and her husband at the end. And she still loved me.

Oncoming headlights bore down upon us, then slid by, one after another. The quiet pulse of late-night travel lulled me to sleep, and I dreamed I was a little pink piglet scampering across an open field. A horrible witch chased me with a butcher's knife, trying to cut off my corkscrew tail.

NINE

*B*UNNY LURCHED UP FROM BEING MY PILLOW, jolting me awake. Out in the flat middle of nowhere the Catfish had pulled into the Okay Corral Gas and Food Mart. The overhanging lights made an eerie glow around the car. The place was like a spaceship.

"Where are we?" I asked, wondering why it was called the Okay Corral Gas and Food Mart and not what we'd learned in school—the O. K. Corral, the location of a wild west shootout with the Earp brothers, but Bunny and I called them the Burp brothers. I like Okay better, being the optimist that I am.

"Go back to sleep, Ruby Clyde." He threw open the door.

Last time somebody told me to go back to sleep I woke up in another state, so I wasn't about to do *that* again.

He slammed the car door and that woke Mother.

"Where are we?" she asked.

But I couldn't answer her, so Mother tapped on the window to ask him, but Catfish brushed her off. "Just stay in the car, for crying out loud," he said. Soon as he pumped the car full of gas, he marched inside the store.

"Mother, let's get out now, let's hitchhike home," I said.

"It's a long way back home," she said.

"At least let's go to Cypress Mill. Why didn't you ever tell me you have a sister?"

"Oh, baby, she doesn't want to see me."

I thought I was the one she didn't want to see, but Mother didn't say that. She went on to say, "Besides, she's a solitary."

"What's a solitary?" I asked.

"A nun who lives alone," she said. "So they can pray and work and ignore family. So you see, Ruby Clyde, Carl is all we have."

She couldn't have been more wrong about that. We had each other.

The Catfish had told me to stay in the car, but staying

in the car was easier said than done. My pig had needs. Bunny needed a walk, but I couldn't find the lasso rope that came with my cowboy outfit, so Mother grabbed panty hose from her bag for me to use as a leash. I tied one stretchy foot around Bunny's neck. Bunny pulled until the panty hose stretched into a tight thread from my hands to his neck. Hard pig toes tapped across the pavement. It's funny how you think of pigs as big and fat, but in reality they walk like toe dancers, regular ballerinas. That snout of his raced this way and that, like a motorboat pulling us both through the bushes.

·········•••·········

THERE WASN'T MUCH IN THE WAY OF GRASS AROUND that gas station, just a lot of sandy dirt and rock and groups of small twisty trees. Bunny did his business pretty quickly, then rooted around under the starry sky.

Stars were one thing that always gave me hope, even with that brain-chilling thought about the end of the sky: it couldn't end—it couldn't go on forever. So what the heck did it do? I still found hope in the skies—hope that answers existed, whether impossible or not.

Out there in the dark, the sky was filled with bright holes like an upturned colander. I had never seen so much sky. The Big Dipper and Orion were the only constellations I knew by name. But I liked to make up new ones: Jonah's Whale, Jacob's Ladder, Baby Moses Floating in the Reed Basket. My very own constellations everywhere. That Texas sky held the entire Old Testament: Lot's Wife, plain as day; the Parting of the Red Sea; Adam and Eve running around in fig leaves. And looking up in the heavens, I made up a whole new story and wrote it across the sky. I called it the Heroic Rescue of Bunny the Pig. There ran the Catfish, all legs and knees, across the night sky, Bunny tucked under his arm. I was proud to have been a part of his rescue.

Just then cracking sounds and yelling broke out at the filling station. I'd heard that sound back at the IQ Zoo. Gunshots.

······•······

By the time I ran to the edge of the light, I saw Catfish bobbing across the parking lot. He held a bag of something in one hand and was shooting his pistol over his head. "Whoo-hoo mercy!"

This guy ran out behind him yelling, "Get out of my store, fool." He carried his own long gun, which he pulled to his shoulder and fired.

It was a real-life gunfight but it seemed like they were playacting until the Catfish, who was dancing and shooting, fell forward on his face.

The store owner reloaded and pointed that gun right at my mother, who stood in wide-eyed fear. A slight breeze was blowing her dress against her legs. Her hair moved gently behind her shoulders. The neon lights overhead gave her a halo. The store owner shook the gun and screamed, "Be still, woman, or I'll pull the trigger!"

"Mama!" I cried from the shadows.

She looked at me with a warning glare that meant *be silent*, then shifted her eyes to the bushes. I knew that was where she wanted me to go and hide. I was so afraid the store owner would shoot her when she moved, but he didn't.

"Mama!" I cried out again, but quieter, like saying

it twice would make a difference. I didn't know what to do.

That's when Mother said, "Eleanor will help." The owner wouldn't know what she was talking about, but I knew it was a message for me. And I guess she thought I could just do that, since I took care of so many things in our life.

••••••••●•••••••

My mind detached from my body entirely. My skin was a shell, and my guts were as cold as the inside of a refrigerator, not to mention my scrambled brain. My feet were glued to the earth, like in a nightmare where you can't move.

Suddenly Bunny began to run circles around me. The panty hose wrapped my legs and made it so I couldn't walk. I swear to God, and I don't swear lightly, but I swear I think Bunny was tangling me up trying to protect me.

You won't believe what I did. I still don't understand it myself. When Bunny pulled frantically on the panty hose, I let him drag me back out in the bushes, past the lights, back into the dark.

I'm not one to do what I'm told, but I did. I hid just like Mother ordered.

I'm ashamed to admit that I let Bunny pull me back out in the dark, and I let him do it because I was afraid. Plain and simple. I was afraid and my better brain wasn't working.

Being afraid was not like me at all, but I had no idea what to do. I have never been short on ideas in my life, but this Wild West gunfight was way over the top for me. There was the Catfish laid out on the asphalt, bleeding. There was my mother looking down a shotgun.

I liked to barf—feeling guilty and cowardly, keeping myself safe instead of trying to protect Mother, but what could I have done that wouldn't have made things worse? Me and my pig. What if I ran screaming up to Mother and got us both shot? What good would that do?

Why on earth had Mother told me to find Eleanor Rose? The woman hated me. Maybe the Catfish was right about stray kids being put in the orphanage. Because what if I found her and she slammed the door in my face?

Then I'd still be alone in the world, without any adult. A voice filled my head. Carl's voice: *They lock you in an orphanage until you're eighteen years old.* And underneath it all, the low calm voice of God, saying absolutely nothing.

With all those feelings and voices and silence battling inside of me, it's a wonder I didn't vanish.

But I didn't vanish.

I sat down in the dirt with my pig and shivered.

TEN

SITTING OUT IN THOSE DARK BUSHES WAS NOT AN easy thing for me to do.

I prayed with all my heart that I would not hear another gunshot because the only gun left was pointed at Mother's chest. And while I could put a lot of bad things out of my mind, that was not one of them. So I prayed, and that desperate prayer sent up a constant vibrating plea to God. If anybody on this earth could have heard it, they would have thought it was the school bell clanging, the one that tells you there's a fire in the building, tells you to get outside, run, run for your life. I don't think God enjoys those kinds of prayers very much, but it was the best I could do. And it was either pray like a fire alarm or disintegrate on the spot.

Prayers and superstitions weren't helping me at all. But Bunny did. My pig leaned into my side until I stopped shivering, which seemed like quite a long time. His snout pointed up at my face like a periscope, swiveling with my every move. He was determined to make me feel supervised and cared for, with a wrinkle and a twitch.

The police sirens swarmed the air. I turned my head to look, but Bunny squirmed himself into my line of vision. He poked my cheek with his snout, forcing my face back to the shadows.

I kept thinking, *Any minute Mother will come looking for me.* I half expected to hear people calling my name, telling me to come out, that everything would be okay. But she didn't. They didn't. It wouldn't.

·········●·········

Sirens whipped around, churning my heart so hard I grabbed my chest to hold it in. Police lights lobbed bright blue ropes up in the dark sky. The excitement wasn't dying down. I needed to see what was happening, orphanage or not.

I mustered my best fake bravery and tiptoed through the edge of darkness in my cowboy boots, dragging my piglet on a panty hose leash, like it was the most normal thing in the world to sneak up on a gas station where a robbery had just taken place.

I crept through the trees until I could see better. They were loading the Catfish's stretcher into the back of an ambulance, but he kept sitting up and hollering, "My leg. My leg. I been shot."

The store owner stood out front and hollered, "Quit that complaining, fool. You shot your own stupid self." And he slung that shotgun on his shoulder like this kind of thing happened every day at his place of business. He had a trickle of blood down the side of his face, which didn't seem to bother him.

A policewoman was putting handcuffs on Mother.

That was so wrong, I liked to died. Why were they arresting Mother? The Catfish was the criminal, not her. She hadn't done anything wrong except keep company with the Catfish, who turned out to be stupider than I ever imagined.

I had to force myself back in the bushes. Otherwise I would have flown at the policewoman fists a-flying. Mother didn't want me to do that. I found a safer, darker place behind a large rock where I settled into a leafy nook.

I found my lasso, the one I would have used as a leash for Bunny. It was right under my nose—literally. I had hung it around my neck and forgotten. Soon as I got my hands on it I knew what to do. I strung out the rope and laid it in a circle around myself and Bunny, just like the bad child's circle in Mr. Upchuck's office. I hoped so bad that it was true about keeping the snakes away. We pulled in all our legs.

The twisted trees where I hid closed in tight, so I looked to the sky again, hoping the constellations would comfort me. But Orion and the Big Dipper, the ones I had just seen, had hidden themselves in the mass of dots. And Bible stories weren't showing up either. They were gone. You know, there was a time in there, when Jesus was about my age, that he got lost altogether. The Bible doesn't say a word about those teenage years. I was close to that age, and I wondered if I was getting into the lost years of Ruby Clyde.

Lost. I covered my eyes with both hands, then covered my ears. But I couldn't do both at once, so I lowered my face between my bent knees and hid. Bunny rooted under one of my legs to see what I was doing in there, but I couldn't tell him. He was so brave and strong. How could I tell him that we had rescued him from the IQ Zoo, only to put him in a worse situation?

If they put stray girls in the state orphanage, what did they do with stray pigs? Bacon, that's what. I felt meddle-some and ashamed to have been so proud of his heroic rescue from the indignities of the Circus God. The whole mess was from trying to get Catfish into show business and Bunny out of show business; but show business—any kind of business—was a step up from the butcher.

Mother had told me to hide, and to get to Cypress Mill. But she hadn't counted on me staying out in the dark with the snakes, wolves, and laughing hyenas. I curled around Bunny and tried to imagine Mother's voice. *Sweet dreams,* she always said to me. But I couldn't hear it.

It was just me under the stars, breathing heavily, with a pig I loved. Some nun who hated me had no idea that I was coming her way. And I had no entire clue how that was going to happen.

Sweet dreams my foot! I didn't need sweet dreams, I just needed to sleep. And I let sleep choke my thoughts. Shoot, I'd take anything over what had already happened on that—my twelfth birthday.

ELEVEN

RUMBLING TRUCK ENGINES KNOCKED ME awake.

I looked up at the morning sky and realized that for the second day in a row I was not at home. Neither was I in the Catfish's car. (No thumbtacks holding the fabric up, nothing but tree limbs and clouds overhead.) Where I was, was on the hard ground. My bones were angry, neck stiff, mouth parched.

Suddenly, I remembered everything that had happened, clear as a bell: my birthday cake, my piglet, my mother gone. I didn't feel one year older; I felt a hundred million years older.

I sat up fast, shook my head, and locked eyes with Bunny, who was sitting on his little haunches patiently waiting for me to wake up.

"Okay, what now?" I asked, but the piglet only sighed heavily.

I stood up and brushed myself off, picked up the protective lasso and looped it around Bunny's neck. Then I saw Mother's panty hose crumpled in the dust, the ones she had given me to walk my pig. I felt a cry rolling up from my toes but I stuffed it back down.

No. Time. For. That.

I'd never find Aunt Eleanor Rose if I just sat there in the dust. I had to get up and do something, anything, even though I had no entire clue what that might be.

We eased back up to the Okay Corral, and even though it was early morning, the place was busy with noisy trucks and cars. A portion of the parking lot was roped off with crime scene tape. Other than that you wouldn't have known the calamity that had occurred. I wished I could have said the same for myself.

Just remove all of it from my brain.

But that was foolish thinking. And I am not foolish.

I was hungry, but first I needed to find the little girls'
room. I walked all the way around the building hoping to
find an outside door to the toilets. But there wasn't one.
That was a problem. I wasn't about to leave Bunny tied
up outside, so I picked up the little fella and covered him
with my cowboy hat, then strolled through the store, keeping my head high. Bunny didn't wiggle at all. He's smart
that way.

The toilet doors had a theme. A painted cowboy with
a lasso for the men, and for the ladies a cowgirl with a
fringy skirt. I pushed into the cowgirl door.

Inside there were three stalls, all empty. So I had time
to stop at the sinks. I grabbed a handful of water and held
it up for Bunny to slurp. I splashed some on my face, then
before anybody else came in I hurried into the first stall.

I tried to keep Bunny in my lap but couldn't. "Don't
touch anything," I said, putting him down on the dirty
floor, and he listened. He didn't lick or sniff, he just waited
for me to do my business and flush.

Then I heard someone else come in the ladies' room. I
snatched Bunny up real quick, so they wouldn't see his
hooves under the door. I waited. The sink water ran

and stopped. I waited some more. I heard humming. I heard footsteps into the third toilet, and when they stopped in the stall, I covered Bunny with my hat and headed out, fast. Deliberate.

Three steps out I heard, "Ruby Clyde? Is that you?"

I almost dropped the pig.

It was Angie from the Hot Springs campsite. She had not gone into the stall for real, she had only stepped in to grab a handful of toilet paper and stepped right back out. She blew her nose and then dabbed lightly.

It had only been one day since I had seen her, but it felt like forever, so much had happened.

"Dear child, whatever is wrong?" Her eyes traveled between my face and my pig, trying to decide which was more unexpected. I must have looked a sight because she settled on my face.

"My world has exploded into a million dangerous pieces!" I blurted.

She saw that I was dead serious so she stepped to the door and locked it.

She turned her back to the door and leaned against it. "Where are your parents?"

"The Catfish is not my father," I spat out. "That stupid fool robbed this gas station and got them both arrested. I hid in the bushes so the police wouldn't put me in an orphanage."

"Ah, that explains the crime tape . . ." She folded me in for a big warm hug. Bunny was sandwiched between us. "Don't worry. I've got you now. Tell me everything."

So I did. And the only good part of my whole entire story was how we got Bunny.

"I knew that man was no good," she said when I finished. It was nice to have some agreement on that.

"Where's home, Ruby Clyde? Don't you have people there? We can call them to come and get you."

Home. I thought about my friend Bunny, but her stepfather was kind of mean; the school nurse was always nice to me, but she had a job; Mr. Upchuck, but he'd put me in the orphanage for sure. My grandmother was dead, and she could stay that way for all I cared. Who else was there at home?

Suddenly, I realized there was nobody for me back home. I had wanted so badly to go home, but I hadn't thought about what I would do when I got there. I was homesick through and through but didn't even know what home meant anymore.

••••••••••●•••••••••

MY FACE IN THE BATHROOM MIRROR LOOKED LIKE IT belonged to somebody else. I shook my head—no, nobody at home, no home. I didn't have any choice. "I have an aunt near here. Eleanor Rose, she's a nun in Cypress Mill. Could you help me find her, please? Oh please. I don't know what to think."

"Okay then," she said. "I'll do the thinking."

I wasn't accustomed to anybody doing my thinking, but I was flat out of thoughts.

"You ready?" she said, poised to unlock the door.

I put the hat back over Bunny, Angie flipped the lock, and out we walked.

"Go on over to my car, it's the yellow Volvo. I'm going to get a map and ask a few questions." She marched up to the counter with the cash registers while I walked out, one careful step after another, hiding Bunny. But I had Angie now, so I wasn't so afraid of getting caught and put in the orphanage. It was a miracle. The whole thing. Angie was an angel, for sure, showing up like that.

I didn't know what a Volvo was, but her boxy yellow car sat by the far pump, away from the crime scene tape. I strapped into the passenger seat and placed Bunny on my lap. After a while Angie came out of the store, got into the driver's seat, handed me a paper bag, and fastened her seat belt.

"Hope you like chocolate milk," she said as she turned the ignition.

I answered by opening the glass bottle and gulping. I twisted in the seat and watched through the rear window. As the Okay Corral got smaller, we took a curve and the worst place on earth was gone. Angie found the ramp and sped up to match the traffic on the interstate.

When we reached a steady pace, I finished the chocolate milk and burped.

And once I had something in my stomach, I didn't waste any time. Questions poured out.

Where did they take Mother? Is she in jail? How long will they keep her? Is she with that horrible Catfish? When can I see her?

"Take a breath, girl. I can't get a word in edgewise." She drew one hand through her loose curls and laughed, a soft, friendly laugh.

"Okay, tell me." I forced myself to quit talking and listen. "Tell me what you know."

Angie sighed and said, "I don't know much, but I'm pretty sure that your mother and her boyfriend are in two different jails."

"Good riddance," I growled, then shut up again.

"And she is a quiet woman so I think things will go smoothly for her."

"What things?"

"Ruby Clyde . . ." She cut her eyes at me. I zipped my lip. "She'll probably have a trial, in a court."

"A trial? But she didn't *do* anything. It was all that stupid stupid Catfish."

"That may be, but these things take time."

·······●··●·······

ANGIE INSISTED ON BUYING ME SOME CLOTHES. SHE stopped at one of those Everything's A Bargain stores and grabbed some panties and socks, a pair of shorts and a striped top, and some blue pajamas with balloons all over. She was a fast shopper and I liked that. She picked up a box of Cheerios for Bunny and said, "Let's find us some breakfast."

She was doing a good job of being the thinker, so I let her keep on.

Bunny ate Cheerios from my hand as Angie drove to a diner and parked. She took me inside and put me down at a booth, then left to get a bowl of water for Bunny.

While she was away, the waitress spread menus on the table and came back with forks rolled into paper napkins. "Can I get you something to drink?"

I read the big menu, looking for beverages.

Angie returned and slid into the booth across from me. "Coffee please," she told the waitress. "For both of us." She remembered I'd had coffee at the campsite. "And water too. No ice."

She unfolded the map and flattened it on the table. "I found out Cypress Mill is west of Austin." She ran her finger along a spidery line, then stopped and stabbed the map. "There it is. Not too far. I couldn't find a phone listing for your aunt but we can drive up there and ask around. They said it's just a crossroad really, but there's a store."

Angie read the menu and talked to me at the same time. "Can you read a map? I'll need a navigator."

"Wordly Wizard," I shouted automatically.

The waitress had just walked up to take our order. She looked at me like I was a bug.

"Navigate." I scrunched my shoulders together and smiled up at her. "It's one of my vocabulary words."

"Okaaay," she said. "Is egg one of your vocabulary words? Or pancake?"

"Pancakes please, with bacon." I thought of Bunny and I got a stabbing pain. "Wait! No bacon."

TWELVE

E DROVE AROUND THE OUTSIDE OF THE city of Austin. I'd never seen so many big buildings. Jets were flying low overhead and landing somewhere nearby. The map was open on my lap as I navigated for Angie. Bunny wound around my feet protesting being replaced by a map.

"Here, turn here!" I shouted. "Go right." Angie cut across two lanes of traffic just in time to catch that exit. Then we headed away from town and up into the hills.

Civilization thinned out pretty quickly and we didn't see much in the way of houses or other people. Ranch after rocky ranch. What I did see were bulls in the pastures with the biggest horns I have ever seen. One of them stood by a fence and he raised his head as we drove by— honest to God, his horns were so big he looked like an airplane. I remembered the cows crowded in the truck on the highway. If those cows had had giant horns, nobody could have ever forced them into a truck. I wished I had giant horns, then the Catfish could never have put me in his car and dragged me to Hot Springs.

I was worried about Eleanor Rose refusing to accept me, but I didn't want to spook Angie; she was going out of her way to help me. Still, I screwed up my courage and said, with some hesitation, "You know, when we get up there and find my aunt, I want to be the one to tell her who I am."

"She doesn't know who you are?" Angie kept her eyes on the road, but I could tell she wanted to turn and look at me.

"No, we've never met," I said.

"No photographs even?"

"There was a falling-out," I said. "In the family, before I was born."

"I see. Well, okay. I understand . . ." But when I didn't

say anything, she squinted at me. "Is something else bothering you, Ruby Clyde?"

I really wasn't going to tell her that my mother and aunt's strangeness from each other was all my fault. If my mother hadn't been pregnant with me, Eleanor Rose wouldn't have gotten mad and left. Angie might not want to take me and leave me where I wasn't wanted. She was an angel and all, but she might decide to take me back to the police and the orphanage.

"I just need her to help my mother, that's all."

"I'm sure she will," Angie said.

But I wasn't sure at all.

THIRTEEN

I LOOKED UP FROM THE MAP JUST IN TIME TO SEE the Red Eye Truck Stop. Over the roof was a giant neon eyeball, and it was, in fact, lit-up blood vessels. A big, bloodshot eyeball looking right at me.

"This is it," I yelped, but Angie had already started to slow.

She pulled in by a gas pump, put the car in park, and turned to me. "Do you want to go in and ask where she lives, or shall I do it?"

I wasn't ready. I didn't have a story for why I was there looking for a nun. I folded the map and pulled Bunny back into my lap.

"Why don't you do it, would you please? But don't tell anybody about me, okay? I should be the one to tell Eleanor, whenever we find her." The truth was, I'd just as soon never tell her. I didn't want her kicking me out before I even found her. In a perfect world she'd let me live there like Oliver Twist and I'd get Mother out of jail and we'd be on our way.

Angie had already swung out of the car. "Sure thing," she said, and walked inside.

Through the big glass window, I could see her talking to a shadowy figure at the counter. Bunny started wiggling, trying to stand up, his hooves stabbing my legs.

"Okay, okay." I opened the door and out we spilled. I had to jump for the lasso and put it around his neck before he poked his snout in a puddle of gas. Around he went, snorting and sniffing. I looked up and down the road in both directions. Nothing but sprawling ranch land. I was from a small place, but what kind of town has one intersection and one store?

I hoped that meant it would be easy to find the nun.

Angie was still inside talking. How long does it take to get directions?

I picked up Bunny and headed inside.

There I saw that the shadowy figure was a big friendly lady at the cash register.

She threw open a smile and said, "Got yourself a nice pig, Sugar Foot." The lady hurried around the counter and bussed Bunny's chin, "Love a pig. Yes I do."

Angie told me the lady's name was Frank. A lady Frank?

All I could think was there we were: a lady Frank, a boy pig named Bunny, and a tomboy named Ruby Clyde. It kept me from thinking about the real problem at hand. Finding Eleanor Rose.

But that was settled right away when Lady Frank said, "Sister Eleanor's a friend of mine. She's down at Lake Travis visiting her benefactor, Mr. Gaylord Lewis."

I made a mental note to look up the word *benefactor*. It sounded kind of churchy.

Frank kept on. "She'll be back later this afternoon."

I got real worried, wondering who said what about me. Angie had promised she'd let me tell.

"How about this," Lady Frank said to Angie. "I'll show you the way to Eleanor Rose's ranch."

"We don't want to impose," Angie said.

"No bother," Frank said, and held out her arms. "I'll take the pig while you grab a bag of feed for him and put it in my truck." I handed him over and Bunny snuggled into Frank's big upper arm.

I was glad somebody thought of getting real pig food. I picked up a heavy bag and wobbled out the door.

·············●·············

HER HUGE PICKUP TRUCK HAD SOME KIND OF FENCE strapped to the front. I'd never seen such a thing. I used both arms to fling the bag into the back of the truck, then walked around front eyeing the thing. Frank and Angie came out, ready to go. Frank said, "Haven't you ever seen a deer guard before? Deer jump right out in front of you. Every day. It's kill or be killed around here."

I didn't like the sound of that. Not after all I had been through, the shoot-out and all. But we were close to finding Eleanor Rose and that was something.

Frank held on to Bunny protectively. "Hey, Sugar Foot, this pig is riding with me. Want to join us?" I thought that was a little forward, but she was teasing me, and clearly Bunny liked her. Frank turned her wide face to Angie, asking permission to give me a ride. Angie made a quick assessment as to whether this was a good idea.

"Sure," Angie stepped back into her car. "But I have no idea where we are, so don't lose me."

"Couldn't lose you if I tried," Frank said. "It's right down there, turn at the ditch, then go past that thing, until you come to the gate. That's that."

I scrambled into the passenger seat. Frank handed over the pig and off we went in a swirl of dust. Ready to *whap* those deer! Oh boy, Texas was a tougher place than I had imagined. I hoped Eleanor Rose didn't *whap* me with a Ruby Clyde guard.

As we bumped down the road, Frank started talking. "You should know that Sister Eleanor is a bit . . . odd. Don't get me wrong, I love Sister Eleanor, we all do. She is a very devoted woman. All of the solitaries are."

"What's a solitary?" I asked, but Mother had already explained it to me. I launched a half-baked lie. "I mean, tell me more about being a solitary. I'm here to write a school paper on nuns." That was a bad lie but it just fell out of my mouth.

Thankfully, Frank stopped me. "Look, girl, you're in Texas, the land of the free. You don't have to explain yourself in Texas."

Well yeah, I liked that. Texas was sounding pretty good.

Frank said, "Anyway, a solitary, it means they live alone. They don't talk much. But they are pretty flexible about it, doing work in the community. It is just that they value being alone and praying."

Frank hummed while she drove. It wasn't far, like she had told Angie, just down the road, when we slowed at Eleanor's crossbar, which Frank explained is a kind of door frame at the beginning of the driveway. A plank dangled from the crossbar with PARADISE RANCH painted on it.

We turned and drove right under it, into Paradise Ranch.

I looked over my shoulder and saw Angie in her yellow box, following right behind us.

Frank made her way up the driveway, which curved

toward a distant spread of trees, peach trees, Frank said. Right in the middle of the peach orchard sat Eleanor Rose's house, firmly on the ground.

"This is *it*?" I blinked a couple of times like it might disappear. "Sister Eleanor Rose lives *here*?"

FOURTEEN

*E*LEANOR ROSE'S HOUSE WAS NOT HUGE BUT IT was strong; built with gray stones, like the walls had come straight out of the earth, right there on that ranch. It had a reddish tile roof, all bumpy. The front porch was deep and shady and home to a few rocking chairs. Red roses bloomed along the porch. Frank pointed at the flowers in the field leading down to the creek and named them: Mexican hats, Indian paintbrushes, and blue bonnets. Hills rose tall behind the house, rocky and dusty with twisty trees.

Frank put the truck in park. I stepped out and put Bunny on the ground. "Paradise is right," I said. I began to think that Eleanor Rose, a woman who lived in paradise, couldn't be all bad. Well, Eve lived in paradise. She listened to that nasty serpent and all hell broke loose. Still, Eve wasn't all bad. Adam was a wuss, blaming her, but that wasn't all his fault, God made him weak.

Angie pulled up beside us and parked. She got out and whispered to me, "Nice digs, Ruby Clyde."

Frank called out "Hooty hoo," and a distant nun popped out from behind a peach tree. A jolt ran through me that it was Eleanor Rose and I still wasn't ready, but Frank waved at the nun and said, "That's Sister Joan. Always checking on the peaches."

Frank grabbed the pig chow from the back of the truck, walked up on the porch, and opened the front door. It wasn't locked. Mother never locked things either; Catfish *always* locked things. I thought Eleanor Rose must be a very trusting person. She lived in Paradise and she was a trusting person—that was two good things.

Frank took the pig chow to the kitchen. Angie and I trailed in behind her, all eyes.

The inside of the house was restful. The rooms were cool and dark with black wood running across the ceiling and red tiles on the floor. The front room had a big fireplace, clean, but you could tell she made cozy fires in the winter because of the black soot on the inside, and she kept wood stacked nearby. The nun's furniture was plain and hard. Leather bound. No fabric anywhere.

I walked around the front room, stopping at her bookshelf. So many books, a dozen or more by Mr. Charles Dickens. Eleanor must have loved words as much as I did. Books! She lived in Paradise, was trusting, and loved books. Three good things.

I lifted out the *Oliver Twist* book, the full adult version. It was larger and heavier than the short version I had read in school, but I could read it. Especially since I knew the story.

Angie stood by my side. "You like Charles Dickens?"

I nodded and flipped back and forth looking at the drawings. "Here's where Oliver asks for *more*." I remembered that was where all his trouble started—well no, actually, like me his trouble started when he was born. Only he was born an orphan, and I was afraid of becoming an orphan. I felt a little less afraid now that

I had found that the nun lived in Paradise, was trusting, and loved books.

We went upstairs to the bedroom where Frank told us to go while she fed Bunny. I put *Oliver Twist* on the bedside table and Angie put my new clothes in a drawer. "This is good," Angie said, walking around the red-tiled floor. "And look, you have your own bathroom."

I couldn't believe that, but she was right. And it was bright with painted tiles. A bathtub *and* a shower.

"Are you still worried?" Angie sat on the bed.

"No, not at all," I lied. "It's all good. You don't have to stay."

"I do have another three and a half hours to go, at least."

"Go, please. I can take care of myself. Really, I can."

"I suspect you've been taking care of yourself for a long time, Ruby girl."

"Sure, I've taken care of myself. Hasn't everybody?"

"You'd be surprised," she said. "But listen, I've given Frank my number, and if you are comfortable with her, I will drive on."

"I'm fine, perfect, go."

"Okay," she said, "if you have any trouble at all, I want you to call me."

"Okay," I said, thinking it odd that people were passing me around, but that was fine with me so long as they didn't pass me to the orphanage.

·········•·········

FRANK, WHO WAS ROCKING ON THE FRONT PORCH, stood to say goodbye to Angie. They shook hands with chatty promises to take care of me. I walked Angie down the steps and to her car. I had become strangely attached to her, since she was the only one present who actually knew my mother. It was more difficult than I had imagined to let her go. That fear of being rejected by Sister Eleanor and ending up in an orphanage took hold again, but I forced myself to look calm. I stuck my hand out like a soldier.

Instead of shaking it, Angie took my hand in both of hers, smiled, then she let go. "Goodbye, Ruby Clyde."

"You're an angel," I said.

"Not hardly." She laughed, then turned, and, with a

bounce of her angel curls, settled into her yellow car. I watched her motor away, down the driveway, under the crossbar, and onto the road. I felt like she was taking my mother with her. It sliced my heart.

I almost ran back to the porch and begged Frank to take me to see Mother in jail, but I didn't know what that even meant. *Where was jail? What were they doing to her? Would I even be allowed to see her? Angie had said these things take time, but what kind of things? What kind of time?*

I knew enough to keep my mouth shut.

FIFTEEN

*B*ACK ON THE PORCH I SAT DOWN IN THE rocker next to Frank. Bunny was at her feet. She began to talk. Frank was like that, just launching into the middle of stories.

"I'll tell you something about Sister Eleanor and those bad dogs, ones nobody could train. She had a way with them."

"She likes animals?" I asked.

"Not really. Sister Eleanor is not particularly fond of animals; it is hard to know what that woman likes. I'm just saying that she has a gift, a special way with animals who are . . . broken and hurt. But she doesn't do that anymore."

"Why'd she quit?" I asked.

"She trained every dog in the county. They all heel, sit, and stay. That nun scared the bite out of them."

I thought about that and wondered why she hadn't had a special way with her own sister. And I wished she had come home and trained my mean grandmother, her own mother. Why would a woman live by herself, go to silent retreats, and spend all her time with angry dogs instead of humans?

Frank looked too soft to be a cowgirl, like maybe she preferred making pies to roping cows. She said her family was originally from Germany, but had lived in America for four generations, settling in the Hill Country. They stayed. Germans are like that, she said. All over the Hill Country, schnitzels galore. I made a note to look up *schnitzel*. Her husband died many years back, she said, and she'd moved into some rooms attached to the back of the Red Eye. She didn't want to live alone. She wasn't like the solitaries. "I like the company," she said. "The bus drivers, the ranchers, people like you."

Sister Joan finally walked over from the orchard.

That nun's face was all that poked out of her outfit.

But it was a face with a lot of . . . something: black eyes, like coal for snowman eyes; thick black eyebrows, like caterpillars; and red lips, but not lipstick—it was like she'd eaten cherries. She carried a small suitcase in one hand and waved with the other.

"Hi." She smiled.

"Hi," I said back, thinking those eyebrows might start crawling.

"Why do you wear that white thing around your face?" I asked. I'd seen nuns before, but they were modern, in shorter dresses and loose head coverings.

She laughed out loud, and hers was a weird sound, like a noisy yawn. I didn't know what it was at first. "We cover our heads for modesty," she said. "Sister Eleanor got us wearing the full wimple. We could wear other veils if we wished, but something about being up here in the hills instead of a nunnery . . . I don't know."

She sat down with us. Both of them lifted their feet when they rocked backwards. They chatted about the peaches, the Red Eye, Sister Eleanor, and the benefactor Gaylord Lewis.

Neither of them asked me a single question about myself. My being there at Paradise Ranch suited them just fine. Texans! Imagine, a whole state where nobody butts into your business.

After a bit, Sister Joan excused herself and headed toward the orchard. "I'm just out here if you need anything."

Frank stood up and said she needed to get back to the Red Eye.

"Wait, what am I supposed to do?" I asked Frank as she walked away.

"Whatever you want, Sugar Foot. Make yourself at home."

She smothered me in a big bosomy hug and off she went in her truck, down the long driveway. I eased into the rocking chair and pulled Bunny up in my lap. I rocked and wondered what might have happened if the Catfish tried to rob Frank. She might have just hugged him to death.

·············●·············

FRANK HAD SAID I COULD DO WHATEVER I WANTED SO I decided to explore the Garden of Eden behind the house. Was it fair to enjoy this place with Mother in jail? Moping around wouldn't do her any good. Bunny seemed to agree so we hiked down to the creek.

We soaked in the emerald-clear water. We waded in the shallow places and swam in the deep places, then dragged ourselves up on the smooth sun-white rocks to bake like turtles.

I lay on my back, water trickling off in streams. I said to Bunny, "How am I going to tell her who I am?"

He snorted. I looked over, his pink body stretched out in the water with his head up on the bank in some yellow flowers.

I practiced what I would say to Eleanor Rose. "My name is Ruby Clyde Henderson . . . the girl you hate." Bunny didn't like that. "Hi, I'm your niece and I need help." Bunny sniffed approval but I didn't think it would work. "I'm Clyde and I'm doing a school paper on nuns." Bunny waited patiently. "Hear me out, please. I'm all alone and I have nowhere to go." Bunny's ear rotated.

We both knew that I had no entire clue how to start the conversation, so I explained to Bunny that I would wait for Eleanor Rose to ask me about myself and then say whatever popped into my head. Bunny blubbered his lips in a little sigh.

When we were sun-dried, we climbed a wide rocky path. They call it the Hill Country for a reason, you know. The hills around us rolled like somebody had shaken a giant bedsheet in the breeze. Tiny, dark green trees dotted the hillsides. Patches of grass spread in places, but it was mostly dirt. And the sky.

Overhead, turkey vultures caught updrafts and soared. I'd seen them on the drive up, along the road tearing at the flesh of dead animals, such ugly birds. But when they fly, they are lifted by invisible strings—lovely black shapes against the endless blue sky.

The top of the hill dropped off like a canyon. Along the edge was a great rock ledge. Beside the ledge a single live oak tree grew tall. One of those low-hanging limbs stretched over the edge, like a diving board. I pulled myself onto it and sat on the wide bark, then I scooted myself out over the edge until there was nothing below me, just the limb and the air and the rocks at the bottom of the cliff.

Sitting out there midair, I worried whether the limb

would hold or if it would snap, sending me tumbling into the canyon. I wasn't really afraid of falling.

But Bunny was afraid of the tree; he made me get down. Like back at the Okay Corral when he dragged me into the bushes, that pig danced around and oinked until I said, "Okay, okay," and crawled back to solid earth.

After that Bunny was happy again. We sat together on the rock ledge, side by side, my legs dangling off the edge. I banged one boot heel on the rock lazily, wishing with all my heart that Mother could see it.

This was a real home.

It might have been the best day of my life, but that is probably because the day before had been the worst day of my life. I wasn't comfortable being so content while Mother was in jail, and that is why I scooped up two handfuls of sharp rocks and squeezed. I squeezed hard until the palms of my hands stung and then ached. When the pain went numb I tossed the rocks away, out into the canyon below. My palms were full of dents and grit.

SIXTEEN

*T*HAT AFTERNOON MY AUNT, THE SOLITARY NUN, Sister Eleanor, returned to her ranch. Sister Joan had just left. I was rocking on the front porch, being careful not to squash Bunny's tail, and there *she* came, driving a baby-blue van up to the side of the house.

I wasn't ready.

I scrambled out of the chair and backed up until I was flat against the wall of the house. Bunny was still asleep by the rocking chair.

The nun got out of the van without a word. Standing there in the yard, she looked so much like my mother that my mind froze up. I had been practicing for that moment, knowing it was coming, knowing that what I said to Aunt Eleanor would make the difference in my entire future. There was an endless supply of clever answers to explain my presence, but then she stepped out of her van and I saw my mother—only with a nun's dress (they call a habit), big heavy glasses, and a tight wimple—and, well, everything I had rehearsed flew out of my head.

The nun in blue cowboy boots stared at me and then stared at my pig.

What I said to her was "God sent me to you." I thought that might be the way you were supposed to talk to nuns.

"Bull," she snorted.

I gasped. "What's a bull got to do with anything?"

"This is Texas, girl. Ranching country. I call a bull a bull when I see it. Don't try to play the God card with a nun, not this nun anyway."

You could have knocked me over with a blinking eyelash. Texans, whoa. And this was a different kind of woman—one that scared me. She didn't act like my mother at all; she acted more like . . . *me*.

She looked me up and down, studying the fire ant bites

and bruises all over my bony legs, then said, "You got a name or should I just call you Bug Bite?"

I was stumped, and before I could say my name she turned away, looked at her peach orchard, and said, "It's good to be home."

Funny thing was, after that, she didn't ask me any more about myself. Texans, you know.

She marched toward the porch, kicking rocks, then about ten feet from the steps, she stopped and pulled a bag of something from a pocket inside her dress. It was nuts, raisins, and little chocolates. She poured some into the palm of her hand and then held it out to me.

Without a word, she waited. I figured she was offering the treat to me, and I did like nuts and raisins and especially little chocolates, but getting some meant I had to push off the wall, go down the steps, and walk over to her. I wasn't even 100 percent certain that she was offering to share.

Still she waited.

I looked at the food in her hand and eased off the wall. I stepped over Bunny and walked to the top of the steps.

Aunt Eleanor never moved. She hardly blinked. Just looked at me, easy, and waited.

Down the steps I went, looking and stepping, a few careful strides, until I was standing right in front of this woman who looked exactly like my mother.

Her eyes glanced down to the food in her hand.

I hesitated, then reached over and took a few pieces. I nibbled, and while the first chocolate melted in my mouth I reached again and again, until all of the nuts and raisins and chocolates were gone.

She didn't smile or anything, she just brushed her hand off and stomped up the stairs. When she reached Bunny asleep on the porch, she poked him gently with the toe of her blue boot. Bunny stirred and smiled up at her.

"Huh," she shrugged.

Without looking back at me she said, "Get my bags, put them in my bedroom."

That's what I did instead of telling her who I was. I got her bags and put them in her bedroom.

All the while, I worried myself silly. It seemed she wasn't going to ask me about myself either. But still, I imagined telling her who I was, her niece, Babe's daughter. The stranged sister. Strange because of me. Funny thing was I had no entire clue where to start that conversation.

It was important that I tell her I knew, otherwise she'd find out and think I was a terrible liar, which I wasn't. I lied, sure, sometimes, when I had to, but I was not a *terrible* liar. I was a good and marvelous liar.

Still, when I came back downstairs and tried to tell her my full name, it was like somebody put a cork in my throat. Can you imagine that? Me, Ruby Clyde Henderson, at a loss for words.

········●·········

WE HAD SOUP FOR DINNER, AND NOT A SINGLE WORD. I don't remember ever going that long without talking. I asked if I could be excused and go to bed early and she nodded. I was sore all over from sleeping in the car and sleeping on the ground. I couldn't wait to get in a real bed.

I put on my blue balloon pajamas and crawled into bed with Bunny.

Then I began to read *Oliver Twist* to my pig. That long version was longer, more words, more of everything. I wasn't sure I could finish such a big book. But I launched into it.

When I got to the line *For a long time after it was ushered into this world of sorrow and trouble,* Bunny stabbed me with his foot.

Bunny pulled his hoof under his chin like the story about the orphan made him sad.

"You're right about that, and it gets sadder. But, Bunny, remember this: if Eleanor Rose keeps us we won't ever be orphans."

Before I got caught up in the story, I wondered about Mr. Charles Dickens, who was dead and gone. When he wrote that book, he would have never thought it would be read by a little girl in bed with her pig. Never in one million years would he have imagined that Oliver would travel to Texas—if there even was a Texas when he wrote that book.

But I soon forgot all about Mr. Charles Dickens. All I cared about was poor old Oliver. (He was a nice boy, but he wasn't like me. He didn't know how to get things done. Adults had to do it all for him. But that kind of luck only happens in storybooks. If there was one thing I had learned it was that you have to take care of your own self.)

Bunny's foot quit wiggling and his breath evened out. I read until Oliver Twist asked, *Please, sir, I want some more*, then I closed the book.

I turned off the bedside light and waited for my eyes to adjust to the dark. Sleep was falling on us fresh and simple. Dogs barked in the distance and something unknown scurried in the yard.

SEVENTEEN

BREAKFAST," I HEARD. FOR THE THIRD MORNING in a row, I had to figure out where the heck I had been sleeping. Bunny was already up and gone. By the time I got down to the kitchen Eleanor had loaded my plate with eggs and potatoes. Bunny had his snout in his food bowl.

Somehow, the idea of telling Eleanor who I really was drifted away. Brains are like that. I was worried sick about my mother, but I created a world where all I had to do was wait for her to come back to me. Her job was to return; my job was not to get kicked off Paradise Ranch before that.

It took me a few days to get to know Eleanor Rose, but her odd ways grew on me. It didn't take her any time at all to get used to me. She just put me to work. Mostly by handwritten note, because she didn't like wasting words.

For Sister Eleanor, thirty words seemed to be the daily limit, not counting prayers, which she said quite often, always playing with that string of beads.

Every day her breakfast was bran and figs. During the morning hours, while it was still cool outside, she'd work in the vegetable garden and ride a tiny tractor around, spraying bug poisons on the peach trees. She might kill some squirrels; Sister Eleanor could throw rocks at squirrels and knock them right out of the tree. That was like me too.

Then she'd come inside for a lunch of bread and cheese and water. She'd do more praying and psalm singing.

In the heat of the day she went to her desk and fired up her computer. She'd sit there for hours, digitizing records for the Library of Congress. "What's that you're doing?" I'd ask, but she wasn't about to waste words answering me, so she wrote it down on an index card: *digitizing records for the Library of Congress.* What that had to do with nunnery, I never knew.

I'll tell you a little secret too. I watched her digitizing those records, and the whole time messages from other solitary nuns were popping up on her computer and she'd answer them. She also did the whole e-mail thing. She did a whole lot of electronic talking. True, she didn't make much noise with her mouth, but—is that solitary enough? I couldn't answer that, because it was beyond me why anybody in their right mind would give up talking. Why, talking is one of my very favorite things to do. It's the reason God made Adam, so God'd have somebody to talk to in the universe. It's the reason God split Adam into two people—so Adam would have somebody to talk to in the Garden.

Anyway, we'd have soup for supper, more bread and more water. We'd chew and look at each other across the table. Have you ever noticed how loud chewing is when you are not talking? It's real loud because it is between your ears.

After dinner she'd walk out on the ranch. Then, after

her walk, she'd hop into the bed and sleep, flat on her back, until morning.

Some days she left for the afternoon, but other than that, we settled into a routine. Routine was very important to Sister Eleanor. Marching through her days was simple, straightforward, and restful. I enjoyed our lopsided ways. I never even thought about going home anymore. That ranch was everything I ever wanted in a place. I couldn't wait to bring Mother there, but I hadn't made any progress in getting that to happen.

I talked about everything except my identity. I'd say for Sister Eleanor to look how pretty the roses were, and she wouldn't even look. I'd ask what we were having for dinner, but she'd swish right by. I asked if she wanted me to bury the squirrels that she killed in the peach orchard, and that was about all she could take.

"You are just making noise," she said. "Don't talk unless you have something to say."

I tried not to talk after that, but failed. She'd hear me talking, I knew it, but she'd just look off in the peach orchard with one side of her mouth curled up in exaggerated patience, like I was a dog who refused to learn to sit and stay.

FINALLY I CHOSE A DAY TO TELL SISTER ELEANOR about my true identity.

She had invited me to walk the ranch, and she had used many spoken words to do it. I thought, *Ah-ha, that's a good sign.* If she was speaking to me, certainly that meant she liked me. I had proved myself helpful around the ranch. She would keep me for sure, like I wanted her to.

Bunny came along on the walk, trotting like a dog. I trailed alongside Sister Eleanor, then skipped ahead through the dust and rock and ground brush, twirling instead of talking. I even found a clearing and did a couple of cartwheels, which pressed little pebbles into the palms of my hands—anything to avoid telling her who I was.

"Child," Sister Eleanor said, stomp stomp stomping along in her blue boots. "What do you want to be when you grow up?"

"A nurse," I said.

She stopped and looked me up and down, like I'd said I wanted to be a Martian. It was clear she was not the kind of nun to work in a hospital. Why, that woman didn't even want to talk to people, much less wash their bodies and dress their wounds.

"I'm a healer," I said. "I do it with my hands. My hands are real special."

Her eyes turned inward and she caught her stomach like it was falling off. She didn't seem to like the idea of me being a healer. Some people think healers are witches, but that's stupid. Then she said, "Come here, girl."

I did.

"Stand here," she said. "Right beside me."

I moved in a little closer. She took my hand and placed it on her belly. "I've got something wrong here, see what you can do with it."

There was so much fabric between my hand and her belly that I wasn't certain. But if you think about it, how could fabric block healing powers? I closed my eyes and relaxed, sending healing through my hand. No adult had ever asked me to heal them of anything. After a time, I took my hand back and asked, "Did that help?"

She started walking again. "Who knows? I believe in the power of prayer, but I have a good doctor too."

I kept up with her, fast or slow. I adjusted my pace with hers. Bunny fell in step too, just like a well-trained dog, but he was a pig.

Finally, I screwed up my courage to tell her who I was, but when I opened my mouth—lo and behold, no words. I walked on a little farther, then I got up my nerve. *One, two, three—just tell her.*

"I have got to tell you something important," I announced, ready to pour out my whole story, get it off my chest, take my chances.

Suddenly, Sister Eleanor elbowed me out of the way. She lurched forward, lifting a huge rock with both hands, and slammed it down on the head of a rattlesnake, a hideous side-slipping monster that was crossing my path. His head smashed under the rock; his long nasty tail whipped around, slashing the air, shaking those rattles. And he spewed out stink like a mildewed sock. Sister Eleanor kept her blue boot on the rock until the snake stopped writhing. Then she kicked the rock aside, examined the bloody skull, picked up the limp body, and turned to stomp back to the house, her skirts swishing against her legs. She skinned that snake and hung it on the porch railing to dry.

Smashing that rattlesnake was a sign, if I ever saw one. That's what I thought. It was a sign that I was not supposed to tell her who I was. Besides, it was her fault, she never asked me. Not once. And that was the last time I tried before she caught me.

EIGHTEEN

$\mathcal{S}$ ISTER ELEANOR NEVER LOOKED HEALTHY TO ME, but I didn't worry about it until the day I found out just how sick she was. Sure, there was a question in my mind—her asking me to heal her belly—but Sister Eleanor never said anything about being really sick, and she was very active when the other nuns came over to harvest the peaches. So I set the question way back in my mind.

When the ripe peaches hung heavy on the branches, the nuns rolled up, all sitting in the back of a flatbed truck. Their benefactor, Mr. Gaylord Lewis, drove the truck and let them out before leaving. Must have been eight or nine of them. The wind blew their extra cloth out behind their shoulders like banners.

Sister Eleanor heard them coming up the drive and walked onto the porch, letting the screen door slam behind her. The nuns hopped out and started scampering about, chattering to one another. Sister Eleanor leaned off the porch and yelled, "I hope you left your big mouths at home."

"You be silent if you want, old girl," Sister Joan hollered. "We're the verbose nuns."

It was hard to keep them all straight since there was such a sameness in their habits (why anyone would call a dress a "habit" is beyond me)—all you really saw were those little square faces. They swirled out into the peach orchard and began setting up ladders and baskets. Then they were in and out of the trees like big brown birds. As the baskets filled with fruit, the nuns sang psalms.

I ladled drinking water from the barrel on the porch into a small bucket, then Bunny and I took it up and down the rows of trees. Some of the nuns stepped down off the ladders to drink. One said, "I'm so glad you are here to help Sister E, stubborn old coot. She won't take help from any of us."

All the nuns wore cowboy boots under their dresses, but only Sister Eleanor's were blue. You could see all their boots on the ladders. One sister said tall boots fought off snake bites. Texas snakes would not rise up six inches to get your flesh, she told me, they would just hit the leather and fall away.

"Don't tease me," I said, but another sister said she'd been hit in the boot twice by snakes and she wasn't the teasing kind. So I wondered if my cowboy boots were tall enough since I was not nearly so tall as the nuns. I imagined snakes clamping down on my knee.

"Snake!" Sister Joan cried, and I jumped.

"Leave that child alone," another sister said and then assured me, "Any snake in this orchard is long gone."

"Don't worry, child," another one said. "Pigs are the greatest protection against snakes. My father always kept pigs on our ranch for that very purpose. Best snake stompers on earth."

After that I kept Bunny by my side. If he stopped to eat a fallen peach, I'd wait. If he trotted ahead, I'd trot along behind him sloshing water. If one of the sisters tried to scare me, I'd just say *ha ha* and walk on. But I was so happy there in the peach orchard with Sister Eleanor and all the nuns teasing me. Some days I almost forgot anything was wrong in the world.

Those women were like a whole flock of mothers watching over me, and they were watching over me in Paradise, a wide-open sunny ranch with peaches growing all around us.

The best part of the day was the smell—ripe peach smell so thick in the air that when I inhaled I could taste it on my tongue, sweet and velvety. I ate one very ripe, dripping peach and made a terrible mess; the juice leaked all over my chin and on my hands and the sticky sugar attracted bees. I jerked my hands away but the bees kept circling back and dive-bombing me. Two hit my chin. I ran around a tree, but they kept up, buzzing in my face. I swatted the air, dashed for the house, and slammed the screen door.

Snakes! Bees! No place is ever totally safe, but I'd rather be in danger from animals than people, that's for sure.

In the kitchen, I washed up, then made a glass of ice

water and sat in the pantry to drink it. I loved a shady pantry; it opened up my imagination. One second I was thinking giant bees, the next it was snakes, then I recalled Mr. Upchuck's reflecting eyeglasses, then Mother at the campfire back in Hot Springs, her beautiful hair falling around her shoulders. My unleashed mind was better than a slide show.

Suddenly Sister Eleanor came in out of the heat. The door banged and she marched to the kitchen sink where she took off her wimple.

I mean to tell you, she was completely bald.

I didn't make a peep.

She leaned over the sink, holding her bald head under the running water, cooling off from the heat. She looked like a giant baby hamster. (I saw my friend Bunny's hairless baby hamsters once, before the daddy hamster got in the cage and ate them.) Sister Eleanor twisted her bald head to one side, then the other, letting the water run over it. Then she stood up and wiped her head dry with a dish towel.

Have you ever seen a bald-headed woman? It's not normal.

There was a song the Catfish used to sing about an old maid: *She took out her teeth and her big glass eye and the hair off the top of her head.* If I remember correctly, a burglar came into her bedroom and she shot him. That burglar couldn't have been any more surprised than I was to see that Sister Eleanor was bald—naked skin from ear to ear.

She put her wimple back on and went back outside to work.

I sat there for a long time digesting what I had seen. The pantry had been so safe, away from all the killer bees and snakes. Suddenly, I didn't give a whit about bees or snakes. Something more real buzzed my face, coiled in my brain, rattled its tail. What was wrong with Eleanor Rose?

When Sister Eleanor was good and gone from the kitchen, I did something I would have been very ashamed of if I'd been caught, but since I wasn't caught, I wasn't ashamed at all. It works that way, you know. I'm not sure why. It is easier to be ashamed of yourself when someone else helps you.

So, what I did shameful was this: I went to snoop in Sister Eleanor's room. Her writing desk looked out on the peach orchard where I could see her picking, so I felt sure she wouldn't walk in on me.

Sister Eleanor's room was almost empty, but the books on her bookshelf told me what was wrong with her. Cancer. The books had titles like *Unlikely Survivors, Cancer: A Blessing in Disguise, The Sisterhood of Cancer, The Cancer Diet, Radiation Poisoning*, and *God Knows Your Fears*. (You know my poor opinion about God knowing my fears, but that's beside the point.)

It all made sense and I hated the sense it made: my aunt had cancer for sure. I did not know much about cancer except that it pretty much kills you dead. That was such bad news to me that I backed up and sat down on Sister Eleanor's bed. Outside, my flock of mothers sang psalms while they picked peaches. Inside, I knew that my life there in Paradise was going to be taken away from me, like everything else I loved.

............●............

THAT NIGHT AFTER I PUT ON MY PAJAMAS, I ASKED Sister Eleanor if reading from a book counted as talking. She thought about that for a while and said no. So I gave her *Oliver Twist* and led her to my bed. I crawled in and she crawled in beside me, plumped up the pillows, and snuggled close. Sister Eleanor picked up reading where I had left off:

> *"I haven't any sister, or father and mother either. I'm an orphan; I live at Pentonville."*
>
> *"Only hear him, how he braves it out!" cried the young woman.*
>
> *"Why, it's Nancy!" exclaimed Oliver, who now saw her face for the first time, and started back in irrepressible astonishment.*
>
> *"You see he knows me!" cried Nancy, appealing to the bystanders. "He can't help himself. Make him come home, there's good people, or he'll kill his dear mother and father, and break my heart!"*

I knew, from reading the short book in lower school, that it wouldn't end well for Nancy or Fagin or any of the other characters Sister Eleanor read about that night, except Oliver Twist; he found happiness in the end.

But happiness was not possible if Aunt Eleanor died of cancer.

NINETEEN

*A*LL THE NEXT DAY I WORRIED. I KNEW I
needed to lay my hands on Aunt Eleanor
again and try to heal her some more. But first I had to
screw up my courage. I checked on Bunny at the base of
the front porch stairs. He pointed his nostrils at me and
twitched. His snout had a ring of muddy dust on it where
he'd been eating peaches all day. His belly hung down
low from pigging out. I sat beside him and whispered
that I had to heal Aunt Eleanor of her cancer, and that I
had never healed anything that big but I had to try. Talking to Bunny was a little like talking to Sister Eleanor
and, come to think of it, like talking to God. Maybe they

hear you, maybe they don't. Either way, you have to carry on the whole conversation yourself.

If only that ranch could have been my home. I would take care of the house and work in the peach orchard. I would go to school somewhere close by and make new friends. If Sister Eleanor got sicker from her cancer, I could practice my healing on her. She would get well and thank me for it. She would want me to stay with her forever.

Finally the flock of mothers drove off with that day's harvest. The sun was setting like a giant peach. Darkness eased into the orchard. The fruit, the leaves, the limbs faded in the shadows. I dragged my boots up the steps of the house and stood by the screen door.

Inside, Sister Eleanor sang her psalms. Holding my fate. When Sister Eleanor stopped singing I went inside and closed the screen door quietly behind me. "I'm back."

I found her in the side room where she did her work. She sat upright in a hard chair digitizing records for the Library of Congress. She didn't turn or talk or slow down her work. She had the gift of being single-minded.

I walked over and stood behind her shoulders, rubbing

the palms of my healing hands together. When they were warmed up I slowly placed them on top of her head. The wimple was between my hands and her bald head, of course, but plain fabric couldn't stop the miracle of healing.

Type type type, she continued, then paused. Type . . . type, stop.

"Girl, what in heaven's name are you doing?"

"Nothing," I said. "But I don't see how you *can* really do nothing. Nobody can. If I did absolutely nothing I'd be dead." Then I stopped short wondering if she was afraid her cancer would kill her.

"Stop that babbling," she said. "If there's one thing I've been trying to teach you, it is only speak when you have something to say."

"I'm sorry," I said, "I didn't mean to—"

"Is somebody else in control of that mouth?"

She was right; my mouth was mine alone.

"Now I will ask you again, what in heaven's name are you doing putting your hands on my head—"

"Healing?" I asked. Even though it was the answer, I felt safer saying it as a question.

Aunt Eleanor turned her head and looked at me like I had broken into her house. She stared me down until I squirmed.

Finally she asked, forming each word slowly, "Have you been snooping in my personal things?"

My mind tumbled down into itself.

"I'm sorry. I was sitting in the pantry when I saw you at the sink. I saw your bald head. Then I saw your cancer books."

"And you didn't think to ask me, directly?"

The thought had never crossed my mind.

"Don't you feel safe yet, Ruby Clyde . . . Henderson?" And when she said my last name, I knew I was caught.

She stood up abruptly and I shrank away.

Was my life in Paradise over?

She reached out and took my shoulders firmly in her hands and waited. I couldn't look away. Time passed and soon our breathing matched one another. Inhale, exhale, and again, slowly. I was so tired of holding on to life all by myself.

"It seems," she finally said, "that we've both been keeping secrets."

I felt it before I heard it. She would keep me.

"How did you know?" I asked.

"Ruby Clyde, I grew up looking at your mother. You look exactly like Barbara did at twelve years old."

Barbara? I wasn't used to hearing Mother called "Barbara." Mean Grandmother always called her "Babe." The Catfish called her "Babe." Everybody called her "Babe." "Barbara" sounded so . . . grownup.

Eleanor kept on. "Even if your friend Angie hadn't told Frank, I would have known the instant I laid eyes on you."

I was too relieved to be cross with Angie for telling my secret. "And you didn't hate me?" The shame of causing their strangeness flooded over me.

"How could I hate you, child, I only just met you."

I was so wrong about everything. All that wasted time but I had nothing to fear. She didn't blame me. She wouldn't send me to an orphanage. Eleanor was family and Paradise Ranch was home to me and Bunny. I hung my head and whispered, "You must think I'm stupid."

"Far from it, Ruby Clyde. Every day I have admired your courage and I have waited patiently for you to trust me. I couldn't just tell you to trust me. You had to find it yourself."

And the astonishing thing is that she was absolutely right. Trust had snuck up on me. For the first time in my life, I trusted an adult. It is weird to get something that you need so badly and didn't even know was missing.

That spastic muscle let go—the one that had gripped my heart when I woke up at the Hot Springs campsite. I could breathe again. My lungs were like dusty closets suddenly open to the sun. Home. I was so relieved that I almost fainted. And for a brief moment, I forgot that Eleanor Rose had cancer.

TWENTY

S IT TURNED OUT, SISTER ELEANOR HAD BEEN going down to Austin to take care of my mother, her sister. So, all that time I'd been too afraid to tell her who I was, imagining that waiting was all that Mother needed, was not wasted. Eleanor Rose had been taking care of things without me. That was the oddest feeling, having someone like her in charge.

The first morning we went down to see Mother, Eleanor got real bossy about my clothes. "Put on the khaki skort, please." She crossed her arms over her chest and blocked my exit at the base of the stairs.

"Why?" I asked.

"Because, how you dress matters," said the same

woman who was standing there covered from head to toe in fabric. "Go!" She pointed one long arm up toward my bedroom and waited. I turned slowly and plop plop plopped back up the stairs, the very same stairs I had practically skipped down because I was so excited about going to see my mother.

Aunt Eleanor followed me, saying to hurry up, it was an hour drive to town. So I scrambled into the khaki skort, stretched into a fresh blue blouse with stupid buttons, then stepped back into my cowboy boots. I thought she was going to protest, but I stuck out my chin and defied her. She shrugged.

"The hair is not negotiable," she said, and snatched up a brush and ran it through my hair.

"Ouch!" I pulled away. But she kept at it until every hair was stuck to my head.

She reached to clip a bow in my hair but I said no, no, no. "Bows are not negotiable. I'm a cowboy hat kind of girl."

"Fine," she said. "Wear the hat if you must, but the guns stay here."

"I need my—" I began, but she cut me off with that hand chop she used to shut me up fast.

"They have no sense of humor about guns in the court-house, toys or not."

During the drive I asked her about her cancer. It was blunt, I know, but since we were all about shedding secrets I needed to know. And I worried about who would take care of me if something happened to her. After all, feeling safe and secure at Paradise Ranch was a brand-new feeling and I didn't want to lose it.

"Are you going to die?" I asked.

"Sure I am," she said. "We all are."

"No, I mean . . ."

"I know what you mean, Ruby Clyde. And the answer is—I do not know. I've had surgery and chemotherapy and radiation. I've responded well but I'm not cancer free yet. These things take time."

More of that time thing, I thought.

I was about worn out with everything taking time, but I wasn't on the committee that set up this crazy world. Sometimes you just have to believe what you need to believe. Right then, she was well enough to take care of me and my mother, and that was that.

When we got to town, Aunt Eleanor knew where to go. She drove her blue van into a parking lot downtown. We entered through a gate that lifted all by itself. After taking a ticket she drove around and around to about the third floor before she found an empty place large enough for her van. Some of the spots we passed were marked COMPACT but those weren't for us.

As she turned off the ignition, I imagined seeing Mother in a few short minutes.

"Is Mother okay?" I asked.

"Well, she's in jail . . ." she said, and I felt foolish.

We walked out of the parking lot, across the street, and into a tall shiny building with at least ten floors.

"This is a jail?" I thought jails were big castles with armed guards in watch towers. Not a big swanky building in town with people coming and going wearing suits and high-heel shoes.

"The jail is over there." She pointed to another building, which wasn't as fancy, but it didn't look like a jail either.

"Why aren't we going there? I want to see Mother." I skidded back on the heels of my boots.

"Ruby Clyde," she said. "We don't have time for this. Joe Brewer is your mother's lawyer. He is waiting for us.

He is taking us to see your mother. It's the only way both of us can see Barbara. He has gotten special permission from the sheriff for us to have a face-to-face visit."

She dragged me a little bit until I heeled along beside her.

"And mind your manners," she said. "Joe Brewer is a court-appointed defender and he is doing everything humanly possible to help us."

I'd never heard of a court-appointed defender before. It sounded like a comic book hero. I later found out that in Austin, the court-appointed defenders are regular attorneys who are paid by the court to represent people who can't afford an attorney. A court-appointed defender fights for the criminals, or in Mother's case, the innocent people accused of crimes. Then the lawyers trying to put them in jail for breaking the law are called prosecutor, district attorney, or assistant district attorney.

Aunt Eleanor rushed me into an elevator just as the doors were closing. "Eight please," she said to a perfect stranger just because he was standing closer to the buttons. Once we were off the elevator the big wooden doors were right there. I thought we should knock but Aunt

Eleanor walked right in. That seemed rude to me, but she did it.

The front room of the lawyer's office was fancy, with artwork on the walls, three chairs, a sofa, a hundred magazines, and a large desk with a lady on the telephone, if you can call it that. It was a wire thing that wrapped around her head and hovered in front of her mouth. She punched a few buttons to send the call along and said into her microphone, "Sister Eleanor is here."

I perched on the edge of a chair and said, "Hey, she knows you. You didn't tell her your name but she called you Sister Eleanor."

"I told you, Ruby Clyde, that how you dress matters. When I walk around in this habit people remember me. It's all they see. They see this outfit and they call me Sister Eleanor. It could be Sister Joan bringing you in here but they wouldn't know it. They would call her Sister Eleanor. I'll tell you a secret. If you ever want to rob a bank, wear a big red wig, the wig will be all they will remember when they try to describe you."

I believed she was right about everything, but not about getting mixed up with Sister Joan. Nobody would forget Sister Joan's big caterpillar eyebrows.

Just then a man walked out. "Sister Eleanor," he said, sticking out his hand. He wore a stiff white shirt collar and a necktie so tight I couldn't stop staring at it. His face was wide and friendly, wise—like a tall version of that little Yoda thing from *Star Wars*. He turned to me and said, "Hello, young lady," and shook my hand too. I liked that already. "I am Joe Brewer. You must be Ruby Clyde Henderson."

Joe Brewer led us down a hall, past a library and a room where people were screaming at each other. He took us into an office with a glass door, which he closed. I sat down right next to his desk and leaned in to talk quietly. "Is it true you are going to take me to see my mother, right now in a minute?"

He smiled. "Yes, right now in a minute, but first I thought you might have some questions." He tilted his head and waited.

Questions, I thought. I had so many questions they were leaking out my ears.

My questions spilled out. "What's a lawyer? How did you get to be one? And what do you do that we can't do ourselves?"

He didn't smile. But I could tell he wanted to. The

corners of his lips tipped up, then he made them stop. "I'll answer those important questions one at a time."

He proceeded to tell me that a lawyer was a person who studied the law. He had graduated from college, gone to three years of law school, and practiced law for ten years.

I wondered about a man who practiced anything for ten years. Had he never gotten good enough to just do it?

It was like he read my mind because he let himself smile and said, "Practice is working at the job of law. Which brings me to what I can do that you cannot. I am licensed to go into court to represent your mother. You cannot do that. I am trained to handle all of the paperwork and procedures before trial. I also know the law, which is vast and confusing to untrained people. And I know exactly how to behave in court. Court is a formal and solemn place. It is a place where we try to determine the truth. Justice and truth."

"That's all fine and good," I said. "But why does Mother even need to go to court? What is her crime?"

"Armed robbery," he said simply, and let that settle.

"But, she didn't—" I started.

"Let him finish, Ruby Clyde," Aunt Eleanor said sharply and I settled down.

"Your mother has been arraigned where she entered a plea of not guilty, and was indicted by the grand jury who heard from the owner of the Okay Corral Gas and Food Mart. She has a right to go to trial sometime within the next 180 days. At trial, the district attorney will try to prove to a jury that your mother committed armed robbery with her boyfriend. After that I will present her side of the story. I will attempt to show that she is innocent of the charges. Then the jury will render their verdict. Guilty or not guilty."

"Will you win?" I asked.

"I can't make any promises but I am very good at my job. I can promise to do my best."

I didn't want his best. I wanted truth and justice for my mother. But he seemed the only path to get there.

I said, "But it was all the Catfish, what's happening to him?"

"The Catfish?" He tilted his head again.

"Carl," I spat. "The no-count boyfriend who dragged

me out of bed while I was asleep and tried to take us to Hollywood."

Mr. Joe Brewer listened and nodded slowly, thinking. I didn't ever remember being listened to so completely, so when he asked me to tell him my story, I told him how I went to sleep at home and woke up at the campsite, how we rode the Duck boats in Hot Springs. I must say he looked right amazed when I told him about freeing Bunny the Pig from the IQ Zoo. I meant to tell him the whole entire story, every bit of it, but I choked on Gus Luna and his gun. I felt *complicit*—Wordly Wizard!—by not protesting, and I had even encouraged the Catfish to use that gun in the rescue operation. I skipped some of that part and went on to the robbery at the Okay Corral. His eyes softened when I told him about being in the middle of all that shooting and thinking they were going to catch me and put me in the orphanage. But then like an angel from God, Angie had appeared.

"You're very brave," he said.

"It's all the Catfish's fault." My chest was tight with fury. "He's the one and only criminal."

"And that is what I will try to prove in court. The

Cat . . . Carl—you've got me calling him the Catfish—will have a separate trial. The evidence against him is strong. I don't think any attorney could get him off. He's going to stand trial alone. And for what it's worth, your mother wants nothing further to do with him."

"That's the best news I've ever heard," I said.

Finally, Joe Brewer looked at his watch and said, "Okay, are you ready to go see your mother?"

"Am I?" I yelled.

"I take that as a yes." He stood up and straightened his tie. Aunt Eleanor smoothed her habit, and out we went.

TWENTY-ONE

E WALKED ALONG THE BUSY DOWNTOWN street and crossed at the light to the big building where they kept people waiting for trial. It was attached to the court building, Mr. Joe Brewer said. And we would have to go through security.

"You left your guns at home?" He was teasing me but I didn't see the joke. And I wondered how he knew I had cap guns and had, in fact, left them at home. Then I realized I had on my empty holsters.

Joe Brewer got to walk right through security, everybody in the building knew him. He was famous or something.

Eleanor and I had to stop and walk through a big Xerox machine. It'd beep if you had car keys or guns. If you got beeped, the guard yelled, "Wand," and another one pulled you to the side and ran a wand all around your body looking for weapons and bombs. If you were carrying anything suspicious, you had to run it through another machine that could see right through things. One lady had all kinds of stuff in her purse. You could see it all in reverse shadows on the little TV screen: pens, lipstick, pacifier, notepad, sandwich, pill bottle. It all looked like skeleton bones.

When it came time for me to walk through the machine, I balked. I didn't want people seeing right through me. I didn't want them seeing my bones. But Aunt Eleanor, who had walked through first, reached back, grabbed my arm, and dragged me through. With that, I made it just fine. They didn't even pull me over and wand me.

Then we were allowed inside. Joe Brewer clipped on a plastic tag that said ATTORNEY. Mine and Aunt Eleanor's said VISITOR.

The thought of seeing my mother again made me

shaky all over. Walking down the hall, I braced myself. My cowboy hat hung down my back; I licked my hands and flattened my hair off my forehead, even flatter than when Aunt Eleanor had yanked at the tangles.

When we got into that visiting room Eleanor looked back and forth between the guard and the door. "Does that door really need to be locked? I mean, we are not the criminals, now are we?"

"Har, har," the guard said.

It was horribly hot in the jail. There was a soapy smell too, like the body odor of people who work in car washes on hot summer days.

Suddenly keys jangled at the door and it opened. Mother stepped inside. I looked down at my boots and then slowly raised my face to look at her. Her eyes did that thing I love. She opened her arms and I fell into them.

"Oh, baby," she said. "You're safe."

I nodded my head into her chest. She didn't smell like Mother, she smelled like car wash.

"Are you happy?" she asked. "Eleanor says your pig is happy on the ranch."

I nodded again. I wanted her to know that I was safe

and happy, but something stopped me from telling her how much I loved Paradise Ranch, that it was the best place I had ever lived. It didn't seem fair, since she was trapped in jail.

I pushed out of the hug, looked at her, and shrugged. "It's okay."

Mother turned her attention to her sister and said, "Eleanor, I can't get used to your habit. Looks like Halloween. Must you wear it every day?"

"Yes, Barbara. I choose to wear the habit every day."

"I'm not used to being called Barbara," Mother said.

"Adjust. You're Barbara, not Babe. It is time for you to grow up. You need to get out of this dreadful situation and take care of Ruby Clyde."

"I've messed up everything." Mother waved a hand in front of her own face, like she was clearing smoke. "You take her, Eleanor. Ruby Clyde is better off with you."

I couldn't believe my ears. She couldn't just give me away like that. I didn't remember ever being cross with my mother, but she couldn't just give up on me, not after all we had been through. I was so upset I barely heard what they said next.

Eleanor grabbed Mother's wrist and shook it. "Barbara, you are talking nonsense."

"What's so wrong with nonsense? The world is full of nonsense. Why am I in here? I didn't do anything wrong, yet here I am in this jail."

Eleanor lowered her voice to a firm whisper. "That's my point exactly, Barbara. We are going to find bail money so that you can get out and be a mother to your daughter. Ruby Clyde needs you."

Mother looked overwhelmed. I wished she had the energy to fight for me.

The side effect of being cared for by someone like Eleanor is that you realize how far short your mother has fallen. I know it had been hard for her. Maybe my father, if he had lived, would have helped, but all my life, honestly . . . adults had worn me out. I was so mad all at once, I almost bit something.

The only thing that calmed me down was knowing that Eleanor Rose would take care of me. I had a home at Paradise Ranch in that peach orchard with all those nuns. To escape my emotions, I went up in my head. I imagined walking that back hill and crawling out on that

limb hanging over open air and not being afraid because it was just me. And I stayed there in my imaginary world until it was time to leave the jail.

······•●•·······

WE STOOD OUTSIDE THE BUILDING, JOE BREWER AND Aunt Eleanor talking about getting Mother out on bail. Mr. Brewer said the judge refused to set bail because she had no family or ties to the community, nothing to keep her from running off. But she did too have ties to the community; she had her sister, who was rich—just look at her big fat ranch. And Joe Brewer was a lawyer—lawyers have money, don't they? I couldn't make this add up. But then again, why bother? Mother didn't even want to get out.

I watched cars and taxis and trucks, flowing down the streets, getting backed up at lights. Honking, like laying on the horn would help anything.

"Are you okay?" I barely heard Mr. Brewer's voice through the blaring car horn. I assumed he was talking to me, but when I turned around I saw that he was talking to Aunt Eleanor. The little square part of her face that showed through the fabric looked like it had shrunk up and turned gray. She had both hands over her belly.

"It's nothing," she said. But it takes a liar to know a liar. She wasn't okay.

"Shall we sit down?" Joe Brewer asked, but she shook her head.

"It'll be fine. Since surgery, it's always something." She tried to smile, but it was not a happy one. "It can wait. I have a doctor's appointment tomorrow. Anyway, we need to work on Barbara's case. I have an idea about bail . . ."

"Sister Eleanor?" Joe Brewer circled his arm around both shoulders and guided her to the bus stop bench. "We need to sit down."

Aunt Eleanor melted into him, her legs listing out to one side, and I realized he was practically holding her up. "I'm perfectly fine," she kept saying. But when he lowered her down to the metal bench, she took a few deep breaths and then said, "On second thought, we better drop by the hospital."

I'll tell you what, Joe Brewer was a man of action. He just picked her up off her feet and said, "Come on, Ruby Clyde." Her head was on his shoulder, and her body, all wrapped in fabric, was across both his arms. Her little blue boots dangled out of the bottom of her skirt. He marched across the street to the parking garage and ordered me to open the door of his car, which was parked front and center in a VIP spot, I guess from him working there.

He placed Eleanor in the back, fastened her seat belt, told me to jump in. I rode beside her all the way to the hospital, holding her hand. At some point she fell asleep or something, because she quit talking and went limp.

She looked dead. I wondered if that was the way cancers killed you. Talking about bail on the sidewalk one minute, dead the next. I worried that we had killed her, me and my mother, coming into her solitary life and tossing everything around.

I leaned into her, searching for a sign of life. Her upper lip twitched. It drew in just a bit and showed teeth. "Can you hear me? Aunt Eleanor! Can you hear me?" Her head rolled to one side.

All that safe feeling I had with her vanished. It had only lasted about a minute. Now it was over and gone. I was back in the bushes, shivering.

I know I said some time back that I never cry, but something came out of my eyes. It was the salt water of a brand-new feeling; it was more than sadness or fear or anger. I felt like someone had sliced me open with a razor blade and all the stars of the universe spilled out on the floor.

I rubbed my healing hands together and touched them to her cheeks. I covered her ears, then moved my fingertips to her eyelids. I wrapped my healing hands around her head and kissed her on the forehead. My healing powers weren't working fast enough. She was three shades of gray when Joe Brewer wheeled up to the emergency room doors.

TWENTY-TWO

*E*MERGENCY ROOMS ARE HORRIBLE. IF THERE IS A hell on earth (and my mean grandmother always said there was), it would certainly be an emergency room. People were bleeding and howling everywhere. Six televisions blared six different talk shows. And the room stank with fear. Maybe I was in a dream.

When I'm a nurse I am not going to work in one, that's for sure.

They belted Aunt Eleanor onto a rolling table and flew through the swinging doors. It is the hardest thing in the world to let go of someone you love, let them go through those swinging doors with strangers who might be able to save their lives, but maybe not. Letting go is not something I'm cut out to do. If Joe Brewer hadn't been holding on to my arm, I would have followed Aunt Eleanor, made sure they were saving her right. But Joe Brewer knew enough about me to hold on tight and make me stay in the waiting room.

I sat down, stood up, and sat down again, then told Mr. Joe Brewer that he ought to call Frank at the Red Eye and tell her what happened. Somebody needed to see about Bunny.

While he called I looked at the other people in the waiting room, but they were too sad to describe. Mothers, brothers, sisters, wives, all with their hearts cut wide open because their loved ones had disappeared through the swinging doors. Just like Eleanor.

Suddenly a honking car skidded to a stop outside the glass doors. A man ran in screaming, "My wife needs help! She's having our baby *now*."

I swiveled around just in time to see a dozen medical people swirl around him and surround the car. I walked over to watch through the glass, but a wall of blue scrubs blocked my sight. It looked like the mother was in the backseat. After a few minutes, one of the doctors turned around with an armful of blanket. The top of a tiny wet head showed with a circle of dark hair. And goo, some white goo. The automatic doors opened for him and I heard the baby cry as the doctor rushed through the swinging doors. Two nurses hurried behind him arguing about the time of birth. One said this minute, the other said it was three minutes later. How important is the exact minute of your birth? On TV shows they do the same thing with time of death. The father pushed the new mother in a wheel-chair, rushing after their baby, but a nurse stopped him at the swinging door and took his wife away.

I watched the father sit down and start making phone calls. He was happy. I guessed it was better to be born in an emergency room than die in one. But I wouldn't want either one. The six swirling television screens made me feel like I was inside a kaleidoscope.

Time must have passed, because just when I thought I couldn't stand it anymore, Frank and Sister Joan flew in like mother birds. All four of us chattered, talking over each other. What? When? Where? How? Until all was told.

After that, since we couldn't control the surgery, we

started talking about things we could control. Did we need anything to eat or drink. Had anyone told the other nuns, or Gaylord Lewis. Where were the cars. Joe's car was still at the door. Eleanor's blue van was across town where we had parked.

Frank and Sister Joan sandwiched me on the waiting chairs while Joe Brewer moved his car to the regular parking. When he returned we sat all in a row, the four of us, in silence because we'd run out of chatter. Our complete thoughts were holding on to Eleanor's life.

Waiting and waiting and waiting. Pacing. Wait some more. All four of us until finally a doctor walked up to us and said, "I have good news." And the breath we let out could have blown the Niña, the Pinta, and the Santa Maria all the way to America. The doctor explained that Eleanor had an obstruction in her bowel, but they had gone in and fixed her. Soon as the doctors stitched her up, she would go into the recovery room.

I was relieved, but I needed to see her to believe it.

"Thank God." Frank began rustling about, readying herself to leave. "Ruby, let's go home and get some rest. She won't be able to have visitors tonight."

"Nope," I said. "Not leaving."

"Don't be silly," Frank said. "Children are little bags of germs—hospitals hate them."

"You don't understand. I *have* to stay. I help at the school infirmary all the time. I have nerves of steel. Everybody says so."

"Hospitals have rules." Sister Joan tried to sound firm, but she was a softie. "Visiting hours."

"But I'm family," I said. "I'm her only family right now."

Frank and Sister Joan looked at each other. Nobody had told them that the secret was out.

"Yes, I know you guys know who I am," I said. "That's why we came down to Austin. To meet Joe Brewer and see my mother."

Sister Joan laughed that yawny laugh and said, "Glad that's out in the open."

I turned to Joe Brewer. "I am *not* leaving this hospital until I see her. I can't."

Joe Brewer put an arm around my shoulder and told the two women that he would keep me down in Austin for the night. "Might be nice for Sister Eleanor to see a friendly face when she wakes up."

Then he found Eleanor's van keys and told the ladies where they could find the parking garage.

Frank scowled and pulled her chin, then nodded reluctantly. Sister Joan said a little prayer and took the keys.

As Frank and Sister Joan walked out together, bumping into each other and turning back, they said, "Call me, Ruby Clyde. I'll come get you." And again they said, "You don't ever need a reason." A few more steps. "Just call me."

I waved and said, "Go home now. I can't call you if you are still here."

My mother birds dragged each other away.

·············●●●·············

MR. JOE BREWER PARKED ME IN THE HOSPITAL ROOM and told me to sit still until Eleanor got out of recovery. He was going back to the office to get some things, he said. So I sat down in a wide chair and looked around. Life-saving equipment was blinking in the shadows. That was all a good lesson for me about being a nurse. The bed had buttons, the wall had buttons. There were wires and tubes and machines on wheels.

I prayed. I made a deal with God that if he saved Eleanor Rose I would do everything on earth to be easy, and help her, and make her happy. I think it is okay to strike bargains with God, if it's not to get something for your own self. I wanted Eleanor Rose to live, that wasn't selfish. Except that if she lived I'd get to stay with her at Paradise Ranch and that was selfish, but it wasn't all selfish.

Waiting alone in that hospital room made me so nervous I fell flat asleep, twirling into another world. I had a nightmare there. It chills my blood just to think of it, but I'll tell it anyway, now that the pictures are flashing in my mind. There was a hideous clown following me and he knew my name. Every time one of his big shoes slapped down, he would sing a letter from my name *R-U-B-Y*, four steps, and then he would stop and scream *Clyyyyyyyyyyyde*. And when he did that, peaches shot out of his mouth like machine gun bullets.

When I woke up, Aunt Eleanor was asleep in the hospital bed. Her lips were cracked and there was spittle in the corners. She wasn't using her nose enough to breathe, so you could smell her insides when she exhaled. Otherwise she looked okay for a gray skinny lady with no hair. Better than dead, that's for sure.

I pulled a chair right up to her bedside so I could look at her face until she woke up. I wanted her to see me first instead of waking up in a hospital room alone, not knowing what had happened. That would scare the daylights out of me, waking up like that. I wasn't going to let that happen to her.

After a long time, she stirred. She snorted in the back of her throat and her eyes opened halfway.

On the bedside table there was a little sponge on a stick sitting in a glass of water. I took the sponge and dabbed her lips. That made her tongue stick out. I dabbed her tongue. That made her smack her lips. I kept dabbing until her eyes began to focus. When I felt she could see me I leaned close and whispered, "Aunt Eleanor, you are in the hospital but you are okay. You had a bowel obstruction, but they saved your life."

Eleanor Rose looked at me, then she turned her head just enough to kiss my hand. "What a lovely little girl," she said. "You are like a song that was never sung."

TWENTY-THREE

*W*HEN JOE BREWER CAME BACK TO GET ME, Aunt Eleanor was fast asleep. He stood by my chair and held out his hand without saying a word. And I took it. He was the only reason I had gotten to stay in the room until Aunt Eleanor woke up.

Joe Brewer never let go of my hand, walking around the long halls of the hospital, through a bunch of swinging doors, up an escalator, through a glass tube, and into a parking garage where we got into his car. He only let go of my hand to drive. Driving he kept both hands on the wheel, but once he parked under a tall building, he walked around to my door, took my hand again, and guided me through two different elevators up to his house, which wasn't a house at all, but something else—he called it a high-rise apartment. I realized I hadn't been outside in the open air since we pulled up at the emergency room door with Aunt Eleanor. We had been under cover all the way from the hospital to Joe Brewer's place. If you lived like that you'd never know if it was raining, or snowing, or hot or cold, or day or night even. You'd never need a winter coat or umbrella or any of that. You'd spend your whole life like the weather didn't matter.

Upstairs, Joe Brewer opened his apartment door and signaled for me to go in before him. I did, but when I walked into the main room, I stopped cold. The entire wall was windows. And out those windows was a million sparkling lights: the river, the park, and more buildings stretched as far as I could see.

It made me dizzy. I thought I felt the building swaying. But after the day we had had, I was dead tired so I went into the bedroom he said was mine, crawled into bed, and went to sleep.

When I woke up the next morning, I thought of all the strange places where I had woken up since leaving home, which was no longer home. Paradise Ranch was as close to home as I had, but now I was in this fancy apartment in the sky.

But then Bunny wiggled against my back and I didn't give a hoot where I was.

"Where'd you come from?" I purred.

Sister Joan had wafted in the door, saying, "Brought you some clothes, sweetie. And Frank sent Bunny for a visit. But I have to take him back when I go."

I hugged Bunny so tightly that he oinked.

I jumped out of bed to dress. When I got out in the main room, Joe Brewer had already made me some eggs and told me to go sit on the balcony, where Bunny was curled around Sister Joan's feet. I still thought the tall building was swaying, and eating out there on a platform hanging off the side wasn't very appetizing. But I did what he said.

"How'd you sleep?" Joe Brewer asked as he sat down with his coffee.

"I don't remember," I said. "I was asleep the whole time."

He laughed but I hadn't made a joke.

Nobody else seemed to feel the building sway. I was

getting right seasick. The only way I could eat was keeping my eyes locked on my plate. No looking at the city spread out below us.

I heard Mr. Brewer and Sister Joan talking about the law, court, and other people in trouble. He had to go to work, he said, and after I took my last bite of scrambled egg I asked him how many people like Mother he was helping.

"Dozens." He shrugged, gazing out over the city like it was a pasture full of clients. "Too many," he said. "And there are always more. We are seriously overloaded in the office."

Mr. Joe Brewer must have seen the cloud pass over my face because he said, "Don't worry. I am particularly interested in your mother's case."

"Well, that's a relief," I said.

He stood up and explained that he was on his way to meet with Mother. He needed to tell her about Sister Eleanor going to the hospital.

"Won't that worry her?" I asked, thinking about my mother just giving up on me, asking Aunt Eleanor to keep me.

"Your mother is stronger than you think," he said. "Besides, she is waiting to hear about bail. We can't go down that path until Sister is better."

I didn't know they were working on bail. "Nobody told me that," I said. "I could help," I said.

"Can you?" he asked slowly. "You do a lot for your mother, don't you?"

"Of course I do," I said. "What's wrong with that?"

"Not a thing, Ruby Clyde. Not one little thing. But some things are best left to adults."

He didn't know my adults. That is, the adults I had before Aunt Eleanor.

Still, I let out a long sigh, which showed I didn't believe him. He put on his jacket and said, "You should know something, Ruby Clyde. I have never brought a client or a client's family to my home. You and your mother and your aunt are very special to me. You are not going to be alone in this world."

I blinked my eyes and nodded without looking at him. My eyes stung, but no tears were going to get out, not if I could help it.

Then he did the strangest thing. While he explained

that Sister Joan would take me to the hospital, he took out a felt-tip pen and wrote his phone number on my arm, right there on the soft vulnerable part. "If you need anything during the day, anything at all, call me."

I cradled my arm, looking at the place where he had marked me.

"Okay," I said.

TWENTY-FOUR

ISTER JOAN SETTLED ME INTO THE HOSPITAL room, then left. She told me that Frank would keep Bunny at the Red Eye and promised to return.

Most of the day I sat close and looked at Aunt Eleanor's face. It's funny how you can get to know somebody better just by watching them sleep, especially somebody contrary like Aunt Eleanor.

I had a parade of thoughts. I thought about her and my mother as little girls, imagined them in matching dresses and ponytails. I bet they played tricks on people. I bet they held hands when they walked. I bet they shared a bedroom and brushed each other's hair. That's what I would have done if I had a twin.

I thought about her baby. Mother had said how Eleanor got to hold her baby, just once—how they forced her fingers to sign the papers that gave the baby away. Then I thought, all at once: *I have a cousin somewhere.* A boy cousin walking around right here on this earth. He didn't know anything about me, but I knew about him.

All day the nurses came in and gave Eleanor shots, adjusted her tubes, took her temperature, listened to her heart. The more I saw of nursing, the more I knew that's what I wanted to do.

People came and went: Joe Brewer, Gaylord Lewis, Frank, Joan, doctors and nurses. Eleanor would wake up, then fuss about something she didn't like, and fall back to sleep.

Joe Brewer agreed to let me stay until late that evening, if I promised to eat. Which I did, since Eleanor couldn't eat her hospital food, but they brought it anyway on a plastic tray. Mystery meat, mashed something, green peas, pie, and milk in a little carton like at school. I ate her lunch and her dinner, which were almost identical.

There is not much you can say about waiting in a room with a sleeping person except—you wait. First off, time is so slow it won't move at all, then *whoosh!* It's over and you wonder where the day went. One thing I learned is this: time keeps moving, regardless of how you feel about it.

Once the sun went down, Aunt Eleanor woke up for real and was wiggly as a snake on hot rocks. She made me shut the window blinds tight and turn on every light in the room. That place was blazing bright. Nothing was right by her—up and down went the bed, on and off went the TV.

She rang for the nurses over and over. Finally, one of them came in and asked her to stop—called her a "sundowner." That's when hospital patients can't stand the dark. The sun goes down and they go wild with fear, pacing and talking. When I'm a nurse I'm not going to tell scared patients to leave me alone, that's for sure.

Aunt Eleanor tapped her bed rail with a deck of cards and said, "Want to play Go Fish?"

She pulled the rolling table across her lap and shuffled. I cut. She dealt.

"My mother taught me Go Fish." She counted our hands, then made a pond with the remaining deck. "It's the only good memory I have of her. Do you know how to play?"

"Might I remind you that your mother was my grandmother," I said.

"Hot dog." Eleanor pulled her cards to her chest and looked at me for a moment. "And you survived."

That let loose a flood of mean grandmother stories, which made us both groan and laugh.

I gathered three books while telling her about having to live with Grandmother after my father was shot and killed. We didn't have anywhere to go.

"I'm sorry, child. I never knew."

"Would it have made a difference? Would you have come to help us?" I asked.

Eleanor frowned. "Give me all your twos."

"Go fishing," I said, waiting for her answer to my question.

"I don't answer hypotheticals," she said, and explained that a *hypothetical* is something that isn't. "That's the road to insanity, all the what-ifs in life."

When Eleanor stacked four books in a row, she smiled like a baby. "But I left to get away from her, not you. After being raised by that woman, I'm surprised I got anywhere close to a church. But I learned that she was not the church. Thank God."

"You left because of Grandmother? I thought it was because of me. Wasn't it my fault you were stranged from my mother?"

"*Es*tranged," Eleanor corrected. "And it was *not* your fault. Why ever would you think such a thing?"

I shrugged. "Give me all your aces."

"Ruby Clyde!" Then she waved her hand over the card. "Go fish, but listen to me."

I drew a card and listened.

"At first you couldn't tell me who you were, then you asked if I hated you. Now you think you are to blame for something that happened before you were born. That's nonsense, you know. And what's more important, you need to believe that. I shouldn't have to tell you that. In fact, even if I sat here and told you that it was all your fault, you should be clearheaded enough to know that's a load of bull."

I smiled. Eleanor calls a bull a bull; that was the first thing she told me about herself. Usually when somebody tells you about herself it turns out to be the exact opposite, but that didn't hold true for Eleanor.

"I'm serious, Ruby Clyde. Other people will dump guilt and shame all over you, and you are the only one who can shovel it back. Promise me you will remember this."

I nodded and she nodded and we nodded together, sealing the deal.

Then I asked, "Why'd you leave then?"

"Your grandmother gave me plenty of reasons, and to be honest . . . there was something else, but that's not something a little girl would understand."

"I'm older than my body," I said.

"Twelve, is it?" Eleanor asked as she fanned out her cards. She knew my age.

"That's right, birthday on the day of the filling station robbery." I made my book of twos and took her aces, which made her mad since it put me ahead. I'm very competitive, even when my opponent is in a hospital bed.

"And that's why I have given up birthdays forever. Nothing but a crummy old day that has nothing to do with me, myself, and I."

"So you plan to stay twelve years old forever?" she asked.

"There's no law saying I need cake and presents and a stupid song. And forget those stupid candles and wishes. Nothing good comes of it. Trust me, I know what I'm talking about."

"Sounds like you do." She drew a card from the pond, which made us even again. While she decided which card to throw down, she said, "Never liked birthdays myself. Don't forget, I was an identical twin, so I never had a birthday all my own."

Then Aunt Eleanor told me that even though they looked alike their mother had treated them differently. Eleanor had been the tough one, defiant. Barbara had been weak. "Even called her Babe," Eleanor snorted. "That's one way to keep her acting like a baby. When I did something wrong, I was punished. When Barbara did something wrong, she was coddled. It's no wonder she couldn't take care of you." I hardly noticed she had taken in three more books and won the game.

"She's been a good mother," I said, trying not to remember that she wanted to give me away back at the jail.

She eyed me. "But you've been the adult, the one taking care of her."

"Not a problem," I said. "I'm glad to do it."

"That's impossible, child. Living with your hideous grandmother and tending to your own mother. You must be resentful, angry, disappointed."

She raked in our books and shuffled until I took the cards from her hands. Twenty million shuffles is plenty. I cut the cards myself and dealt out a new game. As I swirled the cards into a big round pond I said, "I am what I am, and I don't need people to be perfect."

She looked at me long and soft, then she organized her hand and said, "Give me all your queens."

But I had been thinking the whole time about resentments, anger, and disappointment. A thought floated around in my head and I tried to catch it. "Pieces of love," I said.

"What does that mean?" she asked.

"Everything is so mixed up, you can't wait around for perfect. You just have to love what you get. You only get to love pieces of people. Mother has problems, but she loves me." Grandmother and the Catfish, you had to dig deep to find something to love. Grandmother taught me how to get by in the world. And the Catfish gave me Bunny.

"Pieces of love," I said again. "If you wait for perfect you will end up with nothing."

Eleanor reached to her bedside table and squirted some lotion into her hands. She rubbed it on her fingers and up her wrists, avoiding the needle in the top of her left hand.

"Pieces of love," she said. "You're a little philosopher, Ruby Clyde."

"Wordly Wizard," I said quietly.

"Excuse me?"

I shrugged. *"Philosopher.* I know that word from my workbooks."

"On second thought, I believe that you are mature enough to hear my story." Then she told me that she had a baby once that she gave up for adoption. I didn't tell her that Mother had already told me.

"It was the best thing for him," she said. Adoption was a big sneaky secret, she told me. "They say it is nothing to be ashamed of." She snorted. "But they sure are good at hiding it. My mother couldn't wait to ship me off. She hid me away. That's what I meant before. I was punished but Barbara was coddled. She was so happy when Barbara got pregnant. She arranged a fast wedding and pretended . . . Oh, never mind. Her Babe could do no wrong. Anyway, the reason I told you that story is what you said: pieces of love. That's all I have of my son, pieces. The feeling of him kicking inside of me, the feeling of holding him in my arms, the hope that he is well. I understand pieces of love."

I wanted to heal her. So I folded back the bottom of the bedsheet where I could reach her sad and swollen feet. I set myself up at that end of the bed and rubbed the lotion onto her tender soles, between her toes, around her lost ankles, up her calves to her knees. She closed her eyes and made a sound like a kitten.

Eleanor said, "Don't be afraid, Ruby Clyde. I'm not going to quit you. I promise."

TWENTY-FIVE

HEN AUNT ELEANOR RECOVERED ENOUGH
to leave the hospital, Frank drove down to
get us and take us back to Paradise. Sister Joan had put
up a cot in Eleanor's room so she could nurse her. They
helped Aunt Eleanor into her bed.

I remembered my promise to God that I would be easy,
helpful, and do everything on earth to make Aunt Eleanor
happy. He'd kept his end of the deal—Eleanor lived, so
I had to do my part.

All that day, I took up my familiar role of caring for
my adult, asking her if she needed anything, sweeping
the porch, smelling the milk to make sure it was fresh.

But when I carried a hot water bottle into her room she frowned. "You need to go outside and play, Ruby Clyde. Sister Joan can do all this."

"I like doing all this," I said.

But she wouldn't hear of it. "Scat!" she dismissed me with a wave of her hand. It was still bruised by the needle.

If that was what she really wanted, I could do it.

Bunny and I started walking down to the Red Eye each day to see Frank. We'd sit on the bench outside and visit with ranchers. Bunny was real good at making friends. Not a one came into the Red Eye without chucking Bunny under the chin.

"How you doing today, little fella?" they'd say, thinking I was a boy. "Nice weather." They'd tip their cowboy hats and move on by me.

It was there that I hatched my plan to be helpful to Aunt Eleanor. She needed bail money to get Mother out of jail; I needed a job to help. And as much as I hated to admit that the Catfish was ever right, I couldn't be a nurse, not yet. Being a nurse would take a lot of training and time.

About then, a cowboy in a dusty, dirty truck pulled up to a pump. When he stepped out to go inside, I jumped up and said, "Hey, mister, how about I wash your windshield?"

"Sure, buddy, have at it," and he went inside to pay for his gas.

By the time the cowboy came back out, I had squeegeed the front windshield twice, and it only had a few muddy streaks. "Want the sides and back done too?" I asked.

"Have at it," he said, running the gas and putting the nozzle back in the slot.

The glass was pretty clean considering I didn't have fresh water. If I must say so myself, I did a good job and he knew it. That's why he fished in his wallet and handed me a fistful of dollars.

"Send your friends," I said as he pulled himself into the truck. "Tell them to ask for Clyde."

"You got it, Clyde." And he drove away.

After that I asked Frank if I could keep washing windshields for money, so that I could pay back Aunt Eleanor for all she had done.

"Oh, Sugar Foot! Yes. Why don't you wash the whole truck for them? You'd make a lot more."

When I asked her about the cost of soap and water, she

said that I could give her a dollar for all the soap I wanted and that the water was free. "Right out of the artesian well out back," she said. "Not going to drain that one dry, not with a couple of weeks of washing trucks. You use all the water you want, Sugar Foot."

I set up with a big sign advertising my new washing service. CLYDE'S CLEANING INSIDE AND OUT. I even drew a bloodshot red eye just like the one that floated over the store.

Bunny and I sat on the bench out front with the bucket, soap, rags, and a mop waiting for customers. They came pretty steady. Word had spread about Clyde's Cleaning. Best in the Hill Country. And the Hill Country was full of dirty trucks.

The fronts were easy, but I charged extra if the back bed was caked up with ranch goo. No telling what they hauled around in the back of those trucks, but sometimes it took elbow grease to make it let go. Not a one of them ever complained about the extra cost because I did good work. I always have.

It was a long way to $100,000 for bail, but Eleanor had Paradise Ranch so she must have had money. Still, I needed to help; I'm no moocher. And there was that promise to God.

The most amazing wash job I ever did was a really big truck, the kind that has a driving piece up front, and tows a huge box behind it. I'd seen them on the roads all my life but I never really inspected how they were put together. Cab and trailer. We didn't have many of those on the back roads up in the Hill Country. But one day a big rig, they call it, pulled into the Red Eye and almost blocked the sun. The driver scrambled down and began to pump his gas.

When he saw my sign he asked, "You Clyde?"

"Yes, sir, I am indeed."

"Think you can give this truck a Clyde Cleaning?"

"Yes, sir, I can." My eyes got wide as I looked down the body of the trailer. "The whole thing?" I drew out the word *whole*, to match the size of the trailer.

"That might take you a few days, little guy. I have to get going."

He handed me a wad of bills, which was about double what I charged for pickups, and said, "Get that cab spick-and-span."

And the Catfish said that I could never get a job. What did he know? He was in jail, and I had an income.

Here's the thing. Inside that truck, behind the front and only seat was a ledge with a bed. It had a television and a curtain he could close for privacy. I never knew people could live in trucks. That guy was like a turtle carrying his home with him, wherever he went.

If Paradise Ranch wasn't such a good home, I might just be a truck driver, and live wherever I wandered.

TWENTY-SIX

WHEN ELEANOR RECOVERED FROM HER SUR-
gery, she marched into my room and said,
"Get ready. You're coming with me."

"Where?" I asked.

"Tell you in the van," she said. "Sister Joan is downstairs, ready to drive us."

I hurried around, dressing and eating.

After filling Bunny's food and water, I told him we'd
be back. "Don't know where I'm going, don't know why,
but I am going." He sniffed his water then his food and
turned his head up to me and batted his pink eyelashes,
as if to say okay.

I crawled into the blue van and slid the door closed, Joan in the driver's seat, Eleanor up front. Off we went through the hills. The windows were down and my hair blew. Sister Joan's hair did not blow because of her wimple. Eleanor's hair wouldn't have blown even without her wimple because underneath it was just stubble.

"Where are we going?" I asked, grabbing the strap when Joan sped through a curve.

"To see our benefactor," Sister Eleanor said.

"*Benefactor*," I repeated. "I meant to look that word up."

"A benefactor is one who supports us financially. Ours is Gaylord Lewis."

"You work for Mr. Gaylord Lewis?" I asked.

"Not exactly," she said. "He makes sure we have what we need. He owns the ranches we live on and allows us to live there for free and sell the peaches."

What?

What?

No!

"But you own the ranch. It's our home," I yelped.

Sister Joan did her yawny laugh and said, "Her own ranch!?! We don't own anything, Ruby Clyde. We're nuns."

Then she honked the horn as if to say, *The nuns are coming*. Usually I liked Sister Joan's weird laugh but not right then.

"That's right," Eleanor said. "Did you honestly think that I owned the ranch house and all the land around it?"

Not only did I think that Eleanor owned all that, but I practically believed I owned it too. A place that important to me couldn't be owned by someone else. My world was crumbling around me, yet again.

Eleanor told me that we were going to Mr. Gaylord Lewis's house at Lake Travis. Turns out he had been a professional football player. The connection between a nun and a professional athlete of any kind escaped me. Even so, he'd used his football money to make all kinds of businesses, but the biggest thing he did was support the church.

She couldn't get me to respond to her story. I was swamped in misery. More than losing my home, if Eleanor didn't own Paradise Ranch, then she wouldn't have money for bail. And all that money I'd earned washing trucks wasn't worth anything.

"I don't care," I said and pouted. If I could have crawled

out of the moving van, I would have done it in a hot second.

"Ruby Clyde," Aunt Eleanor said sharply. "Pull yourself together. We are going to ask Gaylord Lewis for bail money for your mother. And if you can't be grateful for that, then all I can say is fake it."

I could fake it. I didn't like it one little bit, but I could fake with the best of them.

"And since you are taking this so badly, I ought to tell you one more thing. I am giving Mr. Gaylord Lewis notice that I will be leaving the ranch."

"Leaving the ranch?" I yowled from the bottom of my feet. "Why can't we stay?"

"I will be devoting all of my time and energy to helping you and my sister, thus I can't fulfill my duties as a nun."

"Eleanor, no," I cried. *Leaving the ranch and nundom.* I thought she loved being a nun. Besides, she couldn't just quit being a nun, could she? Weren't there rules?

"You can't un-nun!" I shouted. "Didn't you marry God or something like that?"

"Ruby, Ruby, Ruby," she said. "Calm down. I can and

will quit anytime I wish. I'm Episcopalian, remember. We have our own ways of doing things."

Yeah, sure, I thought, *like chopping off heads whenever you want and robbing me of my home at Paradise Ranch.* If you ask me, doing things your own way is a slippery slope to disaster. But we didn't own Paradise Ranch. Catholic or not. Nun or not.

By the time Sister Joan stopped the truck in the shadow of a giant castle on Lake Travis, I was feeling like an orphan.

·············●●●·············

SISTER JOAN STAYED IN THE VAN WHILE WE GOT OUT and walked to the largest door I had ever seen. What was the point of a door that tall? Did he expect giraffes to visit?

After Aunt Eleanor rapped the huge bronze knocker, an honest-to-God butler let us in and I thought, *Oliver Twist, move over.* The butler showed us into what was called "Mr. Lewis's Office." It was as big as a gymnasium, with a fireplace and windows that looked out on a sparkling lake. Colorful rugs covered the floor and animal heads hung on the walls, all kinds of things with horns. A full-sized stuffed bear stood on its hind legs beside the fireplace. Its mouth snarled open, teeth and all. Black furry arms stretched out in both directions, paws with claws. Mother wouldn't have liked seeing that stuffed bear standing by the fireplace, but I was impressed.

Mr. Gaylord Lewis stood up from his giant desk, and he was the size of that bear he had stuffed.

"Gaylord," Eleanor extended her hand to shake, but he swallowed her up in a hug.

"Allow me to introduce my niece, Ruby Clyde Henderson." She made a hand gesture in my direction that reminded me so much of my mother, I almost barked.

He led us to the chairs near the fireplace, too close to the bear for my taste. I moved to the sofa and sat down. It was so deep that when I sat all the way back against the cushions my legs stuck straight out, boots pointing at the fireplace.

"Sister Eleanor tells me that you have the gift of healing," he said.

I hung my head. "A lot of good it's done me."

"You don't know that," he said. "I believe in the gifts of the spirit. Some people speak in tongues. I was blessed with athletic ability. You, dear child, have the gift of healing. You have it whether you understand it or not. Have you ever thought of being a doctor?"

"Yes, sir," I answered. "But I'd rather be a nurse." I hadn't met a lot of doctors in my life; I wasn't sure what they did. But nurses, they put their hands on people and nursed.

Aunt Eleanor brought the conversation back to her mission. She handed a stack of papers to Mr. Gaylord Lewis. "Here's the bond information you requested. And God bless you for agreeing to do this."

He put on some skinny glasses that rode down low on his nose and read the papers. Nodding, and signing with a big silver pen. "That should be everything you need."

That was it? I wondered how he had the power to do that, but I did not have any such power. What did he have to give? I would have given my life, wasn't that good enough?

Eleanor came and sat close to me on the sofa. "And as we discussed, I'll be leaving the order. This child needs me now, Gaylord. You know what we are facing."

"I understand." His eyes glistened. "But please, stay at the ranch. As long as you want."

Yes! I yelled inside my head. *Stay at the ranch! Stay.*

But she declined firmly. "I need a few months to finish my business, but then we will make room for another nun."

She took my hand and laced her fingers in mine. She gave it a firm jiggle and said, "It is not the number of people we serve, Gaylord. One is enough. This is my one."

I couldn't stay mad at her, not after she said that.

Mr. Gaylord Lewis said goodbye. He pulled me in for a smothering hug. My face smushed against his belly, that's how tall he was. Over my head he spoke to Aunt Eleanor. "Keep me apprised of the situation."

"Indeed," Eleanor said. "It will take a few days, but I will let you know as soon as we have a date for the bail hearing."

As we drove away, I thought about the $257 I had saved from the Catfish and had earned from washing trucks. Did it still count as me being easy and helping and making Eleanor happy?

TWENTY-SEVEN

*W*HEN THEY LET MOTHER OUT OF JAIL WE threw a bail bond party at Joe Brewer's apartment. Mr. Gaylord Lewis had gone into court and told the judge that he would watch out for my mother until trial. And since Mr. Lewis was so big and important with football and money and God, the judge couldn't say no.

At the party, when Mr. Gaylord Lewis strode over to sit beside me, I sprang off Joe Brewer's spindly couch. *Strode* is the only word for the way that man walked. I would have been glad to have him sit beside me, but I was afraid, with all his weight, that the couch would flip up like a seesaw and hurl me across the room.

Aunt Eleanor was in the kitchen stirring a big pot of spaghetti sauce and meatballs made with one of Mr. Gaylord Lewis's own cows, born right there on his ranch. Everybody seemed to like that fact, but I was concerned that he might be eating one of his pets. I had those concerns about eating pork, what with Bunny and all. Seems to me that meat is best bought in stores, without thinking too much about how it got there.

Speaking of pork, Sister Joan came down from the hills after the bond hearing and she brought Bunny. She knew all about sneaking my pig into Joe Brewer's building, which didn't allow pets. She held Bunny up under her habit and marched right in. I wondered about that; Bunny had put on a few pounds but Sister Joan has strong arm muscles. "People don't stop and frisk nuns," she said. I didn't know what *frisk* was, but everybody else laughed, so I laughed along too.

We had everybody together for our party. Mr. Gaylord Lewis, who made it all possible. Mother and Bunny. Sister Aunt Eleanor Rose, Joe Brewer, Frank, Sister Joan, and me. Everybody but the Catfish, and I don't think it is heartless to say that his presence would have ruined the party. He'd had a fast trial and gone straight to jail, did not pass go, did not collect $200. What with him having the gun in his hand and shooting up the place, wasn't much his attorney could do for him. Good riddance, troublemaker. I could go the rest of my life without seeing his silly face.

"You want to hold my pig?" I asked Mr. Gaylord Lewis. I didn't want him to think me rude for jumping off the couch just as he was coming to sit beside me. He took Bunny in his big lap and scratched. "Good pig," he said. "Look at those eyes. He's going to grow into a fine big pig. You might win a blue ribbon at the state fair with this one."

I hadn't thought of Bunny being a prize-winning pig. That might be fun if he wanted to do it later. What struck me, though, was him telling me that Bunny was going to be one of those huge hogs at the fair. He was already on his way. Now he'd never fit in that stupid toy Cadillac back in Hot Springs. I wondered if that circus family had gotten another tiny pig to torture.

Mother was in the shower at Joe Brewer's and she'd been in there a long time. I didn't blame her. Aunt Eleanor told me, after the fact, that people in jail take cold showers in groups. I'd just as soon stay dirty.

Frank and Sister Joan laughed together in nearby chairs. Frank was telling Red Eye Truck Stop stories. Sister Joan is one of those people whose feet fly out forward when they laugh. Joe Brewer stood out on his terrace with the doors open, looking over the city lights.

The building still made me dizzy. I wasn't about to walk out on a terrace of a swaying building.

Mother stepped back into the room with us, her beautiful hair wet and freshly combed. She had on the dress she'd been wearing when they arrested her, the one with the pink flowers. The sandals too. The same shoe that got knocked off at the IQ Zoo so long ago. I realized that she didn't have any other clothes.

Over pet cow spaghetti, I asked if Mother could get the rest of her stuff out of the Catfish's car. Joe Brewer said no, the car and everything in it was "being held as evidence."

"My stuff isn't evidence. I want it back."

"The state usually keeps it all," Joe Brewer said.

"Why? What do they need with our stuff?" I wanted my Wordly Wizard workbooks, at least.

"Why is not something you ask the bureaucrats," Mr. Gaylord Lewis said. I'd learned that Mr. Gaylord Lewis was a benefactor and that was a good thing, but I didn't know the word *bureaucrats*. Didn't sound good, the way he said it.

Sister Joan marched out of the kitchen with a bakery cake. She placed it on the table in front of Mother, the guest of honor, I suppose. For just a split second I thought that she might light a candle and have us sing Happy Birthday, but that's not the kind of party it was. On top of the cake, the baker had written in blue icing, PRAISE THE LORD.

Amen, everybody said, and I was glad to praise the Lord, but it seemed that we should be praising Mr. Gaylord Lewis. He was the one with power and money, and he came down out of the hills to free my mother. I guess you could say that the Lord sent us Mr. Gaylord Lewis, and I was glad of it.

TWENTY-EIGHT

WE SPENT THE NIGHT AT JOE BREWER'S apartment so we could go shopping in Austin before driving back up to Paradise. Mother needed new clothes.

Bunny stayed in the van, sprawled across the backseat, while we went in the store. That pig could sleep anywhere.

I'd never spent time in a ladies' dress shop, and from the look of it, neither had Joe Brewer. The two of us sat upright on a stiff little bench while Eleanor Rose helped my mother in the dressing room. Joe Brewer straightened his tie a couple of times, even though it looked just fine. A lady customer walked out in a slip and asked the sales clerk to get her a dress in another size. Joe Brewer liked to burst, throwing his eyes away so he wouldn't be a party to seeing her walking around in her slip. But she was covered up just fine. I always wonder why you can't walk around in slips or pajamas but you can sit out at the pool in string bikinis. Makes no sense to me.

"Voilà!" Eleanor Rose stepped from the dressing rooms into the area with mirrors, where we had been viewing the dresses and giving the thumbs-up or thumbs-down. Clearly, Eleanor liked the next dress. She spread her arms like she was introducing royalty.

Around the corner glided my mother. Cinderella. I could practically see the bluebirds flying around her head with buttons and ribbons. The dress was lovely, not to my liking, very girly, but lovely on her. And she glowed all over, like that dress had gone deep in her soul and lit a candle.

Joe Brewer gave a thumbs-up, then lifted his other thumb too. Double thumbs-up. I did too, and Mother liked getting four thumbs up.

Then the sales lady said, "This model comes in a mother-daughter option."

What the heck was a mother-daughter option? Well, believe it or not, some people make matching dresses for mothers and daughters to wear. The blood dropped out of my face. They'd tried to get me in a dress back in the department store but I had flat refused. Me and dresses are wrong, flat wrong.

End of story.

But Mother. There she stood as pretty as I had ever seen her, wanting with all her heart for us to wear matching dresses. They said I needed one dress for special occasions. They said I needed to look good in court, otherwise the judge would think I wasn't being cared for.

"You need to look like a young lady," said Joe Brewer.

"Come on, baby." Mother reached one lovely hand out to me and I caved.

I let them take me back to the dressing room and put me in that girly dress, identical to the one that Mother wore, only it was much lovelier on Mother, with her long hair and her graceful arms. I let them pull that thing over my head, button up the back and fluff the skirt.

The sales lady said that the dress wouldn't need any alterations.

I said, "Wordly Wizard." *Alteration* was one of my vocabulary words. Nobody was listening to me.

They walked me back out to the viewing area and proudly showed me to Joe Brewer. I don't know what his face showed because I kept my eyes trained on the carpet. I'd been through worse, I thought.

Then the sales lady hurried over and slapped a silly bow on top of my head. It clipped to what used to be my bangs, but were growing out crooked. Eleanor Rose smoothed my hair out of my face and said that she'd trim it up later.

Slowly I raised my eyes and looked at myself in the mirror. The mirrors, I should say, there were a bunch of mirrors that were so situated they reflected me over and over. I saw hundreds of Ruby Clydes going out into forever, looking absolutely ridiculous.

I turned around to my audience. Mother, Eleanor, Joe Brewer, and the sales clerk. "Fine," I said. "But the boots stay."

............●●●●●●●............

ON THE WAY BACK HOME TO PARADISE IN THE BLUE van, Mother sat up front, watching the rolling hills mound and rise as Eleanor drove toward Cypress Mill. Bunny sat up in my lap and looked out the window too. If he'd been a dog he would have barked at the Longhorns along the fences.

Suddenly Mother said, "I don't deserve your kindness."

"Don't be silly, Barbara."

Then lickety-split, Mother opened the glove compartment, snatched out a pair of scissors, pulled her hair into a ponytail, and cut it all off. Just like that.

Aunt Eleanor and I both yelped.

"I want to be like my sister," Mother said. I thought, cruelly, that it would take a lot more than cutting off her hair to be like Aunt Eleanor. But that wasn't fair.

"Barbara!" Eleanor shouted as she pulled off the road and slammed the blue van into park. She swiveled and burned holes in Mother with those eyes of hers. She knew how to use them.

"What?" Mother said. "You don't like it?"

"Barbara, get a hold of yourself. You can't count on me to take care of you and Ruby Clyde forever. I am very, very sick."

Cancers could kill you, I knew that, and I had been

with her in the hospital, but I kept putting her illness out of my mind. The thought of losing her was unbearable. Besides, I'd made a deal with God. He'd kept her alive for me.

"You can't die," Mother said. "It's not right."

"And you shouldn't be on trial for armed robbery, Barbara. But you are. You'll be home with us after the trial. So it falls to me to teach you how to take care of Ruby Clyde. I'm going to have to train you."

Mother wasn't insulted. She just sighed and said, "Whatever you say."

"I'll hold you to that," Eleanor warned.

TWENTY-NINE

E DROVE UP TO PARADISE IN LATE AFTER-
noon, just as the sun was dancing around
the hilltops behind the house. "This is where you have
been living all these years?" Mother asked.

Paradise Ranch warmed my heart every time I came
through the peach trees and saw the gray stone house, a
cool shady place to rest from the Texas sun. Even after
learning that Aunt Eleanor didn't own the ranch, I still
loved it and wanted to call it home. I looked at it through
Mother's eyes, remembered the day Frank had driven me
out to the place, and wished that we never had to leave.
But wishing comes to no good in the end.

Mother and Eleanor carried their bags up to the porch and into the house.

Bunny and I scrambled out of the blue van. I stretched like a starfish while Bunny put out his front hooves and stretched long, like a dog. *The city is okay,* we thought, *but this is where we belong.*

When I walked into the kitchen to get pig chow for Bunny, Eleanor was setting out food. Mother sat at the table, still in a bit of a daze, her newly chopped hair all lopsided. She really had been through so much, what with getting arrested and staying in jail so long until we could get her out, and suddenly being out, buying new clothes and landing in Paradise. Who could blame her for being in a daze?

Eleanor, that's who.

"Get up, Barbara. You need to wash and chop these vegetables."

Mother looked down at her hands as if they might do it by themselves. I didn't remember a single time Mother made anything in the kitchen. My mean grandmother cooked for us and when she died I took it up. I could make grilled cheese and I could fry an egg just fine. Canned soup worked for vegetables and I even learned to make salad with iceberg lettuce and bottled ranch dressing. Who'd a ever thought I'd end up living on a ranch, and by the way I couldn't see that ranch dressing—white and lumpy—had anything at all to do with a real ranch.

When Mother hesitated, I jumped in and said, "I can do it. I cook all the time."

Aunt Eleanor lined all the squash and tomatoes up on the counter and said, "I know you cook, Ruby Clyde, and everything else that a mother should do. But I'm going to teach your mother how to behave like a mother. Stand up, Barbara," she said firmly. And Mother obeyed.

I scooped a jar of piglet chow, and as I headed out I heard Eleanor explaining the importance of properly washing vegetables before you eat them. My mean grand-mother had taught me that much. Eleanor must have learned it from her; she was their mother after all. Grand-mother must have taught them the same things she taught me. Had Mother known this and forgotten, or had she never known? Was Aunt Eleanor right that Mother had always been babied? I don't remember my mean grandmother ever asking Mother to do anything, always me. I was more like Aunt Eleanor, if you think about it. I had the strangest thought that I might be the baby that Eleanor gave away . . . but that's entirely impossible. Eleanor wouldn't have left me at home; she gave her baby up for adoption, and besides, he was a boy. And more than all that, Mother loved me too much. I knew that even when I was cross with her.

Once outside on the porch, I poured the pellets into Bunny's dish and filled the water bowl from the spigot. I noticed that I'd need to get bigger dishes for Bunny. He'd outgrown the little bowls.

From inside I heard Eleanor say, "Do you honestly call this clean? You don't just run it under the water. Use this scrub brush."

Bunny pointed his snout up at me as if asking what was happening. I suspect he had been harshly trained to drive that Cadillac back at the IQ Zoo.

"Don't worry, Bun. You are just fine—a free little pig. I'll take care of you. All you have to do is eat and sleep and roll around in the sun. That's your job."

AFTER DINNER, ELEANOR SAT US DOWN ON THE FRONT porch and cut our hair. She evened Mother's up and gave mine a trim. She swept the hair off the porch while we went upstairs to shower and get ready for bed.

Aunt Eleanor asked if we would like to watch a little television, a nature show. I didn't know she had a television until she rolled it out of the closet and plugged it in. She adjusted these things on top that she called an antenna until the screen came clear.

It was a show about giraffes. A mother giraffe gave birth on television. It was nerve-racking because her legs were so long. That baby would drop ten feet. The mother giraffe stood there by the fence, her legs planted, and she pushed and pushed, her head bobbing. This big balloon came out of her. You could see some tangled-up shape inside the balloon, and the zookeeper was yelling, "There's the leg! There's the nose." The balloon got stretched bigger and bigger, like a giant teardrop. Then it snapped and fell to the ground.

The baby giraffe tore out of the wet bag and flailed around in the sand. The mother licked the baby, who was trying to stand up on those spindly legs, his knees like basketballs. But he collapsed over and over. After about a minute the little fellow pulled himself up on all four feet, wobbling and weaving, legs splayed.

Here's the question: how did he know to stand up, soon as he was born? That's what I wanted to know.

·········●●●●●·········

ELEANOR BUSIED HERSELF IN A FLURRY OF ACTIVITIES: keeping track of Joe Brewer and the trial, digitizing records for the Library of Congress, and training Mother. The woman gave new meaning to faith, but she was a nun after all, so faith was her business. Bunny was my constant friend, and we pretty much stayed out of her way.

She banged away at her computer, humming to herself. Joe Brewer had asked her to research some legal things. Sentence fragments slipped out of her mouth. *Didn't see that—Oh for crying—just as I—really, some people.*

Every day, she'd walk down to Frank's to use the telephone. A constitutional, she called it, meaning exercise, and she'd force Mother to walk with her. Mother had to learn to take care of her health, she said. She'd walk down the long drive, her habit swirling in the dust. Mother followed, taking two steps for every one of hers.

For a while my mind wouldn't rest enough to allow me to read *Oliver Twist*. I warded off the worries by watching television. And like Eleanor Rose, I enjoyed the nature shows. All that nature could engage my whole mind. At least I wasn't alone in the jungle. Lions were not going to spring out and eat me. That's something.

One week all they showed was fish, things that live on the ocean bottom: crabs, octopuses, flounders. Did you know flounders are born with eyes on both sides, but since they lie on the sand so long, one eye wanders around to the top so it can be with the other eye?

I'll tell you something else too. If you go down deep enough in the ocean you will find fish that make their own lights. Live things can get used to all kinds of situations, but it takes time and terrible need. Like the need to get your eyeball out of the sand. Or the need to see through endless dark.

············●●●●●●●●●···

JOE BREWER VISITED OFTEN. WE ALWAYS KNEW HE was arriving because Bunny would suddenly jump up and run around in circles, chasing his tail like a dog. Bunny knew a good man when he met him.

Joe Brewer's visits always calmed me because he was hopeful about Mother's chances in court. He really believed that we had the law on our side. He believed that they needed hard evidence to find Mother guilty of armed robbery. And they didn't have that. She wasn't even an accomplice, since she'd had no idea that the Catfish planned to go into the Okay Corral and shoot them up.

But one evening, after sharing a soup that Mother cooked all by herself (Eleanor had even taught her how to make homemade bread to go with the soup), Joe Brewer began to share his growing concern. He'd been filing motions all summer—a motion is what a lawyer does before trial. He'd asked the judge to throw the case out because they didn't have any evidence. But the prosecutor said she was working on a witness list, and Joe Brewer couldn't imagine who, besides the filling station owner, would be on the list.

"I can be a witness," I said. "I can, I was there."

"No!" they all said in unison.

Joe Brewer saw all that yelling made me uncomfortable, so he reminded me that we had already talked about that. "Thankfully, the prosecutor doesn't know you were present during the crime, and we'd just as soon keep it that way. We don't want to give the judge any reason to think your mother is unfit."

"Why would he think that?" I asked, but I knew. I was a minor child at the scene of a violent crime. Mother's face had fallen into a deep sadness. I reached for her hand and said, "She loves me." And I tried to forget that she let the Catfish drag us across the country like that.

THIRTY

*E*LEANOR SET ABOUT TEACHING MOTHER THE basics of life. That's what she said: the basics of life. Apparently I already knew the basics of life because she insisted I not do things like laundry, so Mother could be a mother. One time I found Mother out back in the sun, pinning my socks to the clothesline. I sat on the steps and watched her. A gentle breeze swirled her summer dress and I realized that a part of me wanted so badly to let her take care of me. But my heart couldn't let go.

One day, as the three of us rocked on the porch, Eleanor Rose said, "We need to see about getting Ruby Clyde in school."

"School!" I cried. Bunny rocked his head up at my distress, then lolled back onto the floorboards.

"Yes, Ruby Clyde. We have schools here. Just down the road toward Johnson City."

I hadn't thought of that. And I do, so hard, try to think of everything.

"But it's still summer. I feel like school just let out." School hadn't actually let out for me. It was about to let out when they dragged me out of bed and across the country in the middle of the night.

"They start up the last week of August," she said.

"It's not August," I said.

"Yes it is," she said.

"I don't wanna," I revolted. "What would I do with Bunny while I'm at school?" At that Bunny rolled up on his haunches and waited for the answer.

"I don't care." Eleanor Rose resisted his charms. She turned to Mother and said, "Barbara, as a mother, do you want to step in here?"

Mother had never had a hand in my schooling before, but she looked at me and said, "Eleanor is right. I should have thought of it myself. You need to go to school."

"But I need to help around here," I begged.

Mother rocked back and forth, twice, then said, "You want to help. You can go to school."

Aunt Eleanor smiled as big a smile as I have ever seen from her. It almost burst out of the little square nun hat. She said, "Registration is next week. We'll need to get Ruby Clyde's health records. Are her shots up-to-date?"

Mother wouldn't have known that. Grandmother always took me to the doctor.

"Certainly you had her vaccinated. Barbara? Tell me you've had this child vaccinated." Then she turned to me and asked if I had been in public school.

I had.

"Good, then she has had all of her shots. We just need to get the records. Who was your doctor?"

But I knew Mother wouldn't know that. I hardly remembered the place Grandmother had taken me.

"The school nurse back home is my friend. She helped me after Grandmother died. I bet she has all my information." But it felt weird to say back home. It had long since quit feeling like home.

Eleanor turned to Mother and instructed her to locate

the number of the school nurse and call to request my records. "If you need help, let me know. But I think you can do it yourself."

"When you talk to the nurse," I said, "would you tell her I said hi and that I'm okay and ask her to tell my friend Bunny that I'm sorry I left without saying goodbye?"

"Of course," Mother said, then she rocked rocked rocked, and cleared her throat. "Ruby Clyde, I need to say something."

"Okay." I waited.

"I am sorry, deeply sorry for everything. I should never have let this happen to you."

"Okay," I said, a little embarrassed by her feelings and also for mine. But still, I was glad she said it.

THIRTУ-ONE

J DON'T KNOW HOW LONG IT TOOK AUNT ELEANOR to teach Mother to drive. It was days and days of watching them buck down the long drive to the crossbar, turn toward the Red Eye, and weave along the big road. At least once, I heard an oncoming car honk long and angry. She must have been driving down the middle of the road.

Mother was driving.

Imagine that.

Eleanor Rose used every dog-training skill she ever had to keep Mother from running into a ditch, or into a telephone pole, or through the fence and across the pasture. Eleanor was a woman of great faith.

The first time they invited me to ride with them, I said, "What about her driver's license?" I remembered she never had one back home. Mean Grandmother drove us everywhere, and after that I had to bike to the store and school. "What if a policeman stops us?"

"We've got my driver's license," Eleanor said. "Other than the wimple and glasses, they will never know the difference." They both laughed, remembering a time when they could fool everybody. "But don't worry, everybody up here knows my blue van. You won't get pulled over."

I was less worried about getting pulled over and more worried about running off the road, through the fence, and into a Longhorn bull. I couldn't think of a good reason to stay back, but Bunny was no fool, he flat refused to get in the van with Mother behind the wheel. He peered up at her, then twirled and trotted back to the porch, where he flopped down between the rocking chairs. There are certain advantages to being a pig.

We made it safely to the Red Eye, and in time, Mother and I made the trip by ourselves, Aunt Eleanor standing on the porch waving proudly as we rolled away.

Most mornings, Mother would drive in silence. Eleanor had shown her how to drive a few extra miles past the Red Eye. She hadn't seen as much of the Hill Country as I had and she was still absorbing the stark beauty of the rocks and twisty trees. Looked like photos of the Holy Land, she said.

Once my medical records came in the mail, Eleanor taught Mother how to make an appointment to get the rest of my shots and how to register me for school. That was a bit ambitious, if you ask me, but they didn't ask me.

The next thing I knew we were driving down to the city, Mother at the wheel, no less, all the way down the highway for an hour and into town, stoplights and all. Aunt Eleanor sat up front and wasn't the least bit frightened, not even when Mother stopped at the green light and almost went through the red. In a calm voice Aunt Eleanor started to give her directions long before the intersections, saying *red means stop, green means go*, instead of assuming Mother was on top of it.

We parked in front of the clinic. Mother had to back out and come in straighter, and then all of us got out and walked in the clinic door. Aunt Eleanor expected Mother to handle all of the talking and paperwork, which she did just fine. She was even conversational with the doctors, nurses, and receptionist. Eleanor had given her some topics to discuss: the weather, my school, peaches.

I got two shots in my bottom, because the nurse said my arms were too skinny. I didn't like that at all. Not the shots, and not being called scrawny. But I didn't say a word.

I marveled as Mother pulled out my medical records and made sure the doctor updated my shot report and signed his name. She thanked everybody personally and took my arm to leave.

Eleanor had that little thin-lipped smile all the way to the van. I wouldn't have been surprised if she had given Mother a dog treat as a reward, but she didn't.

A few days later Eleanor gave Mother directions to the school so that Mother could visit and make sure I was registered properly. Eleanor looked over the papers and nodded. Again, she stood proudly on the porch and waved as we drove away from the peach trees, to find what would be my new school. As we passed under the Paradise Ranch sign, Mother laughed and said, "Look at us. I feel like I'm going to school to take a final exam."

She was, and she passed.

THIRTY-TWO

INALLY, FOR THE FIRST TIME SINCE WAKING UP in Hot Springs, I felt harmony. How did that happen? We had healed. All of us from different wounds.

I believe places can heal. I believe science can heal. I believe God can heal. And I believe my hands can heal. It is best to use all of the above to get maximum results.

We'd fallen into a pattern of eating dinner early, then walking up to the top of the hill to watch the sun set. Sometimes I'd walk with them; other times Bunny and I would skip ahead, then circle back to catch some of their conversation, then bolt ahead again.

They talked a lot about my mean grandmother,

who was, of course, their mother. Imagine having a mean mother. I'd rather have a felon for a mother than a mean one.

I bolted forward, then crossed the creek, leaving wet footprints on the stone path as we set out on our daily walk. I walked to the top of the hill. Bunny lagged behind, herding Mother and Eleanor to the top.

Nature kept happening all around me, just like all we needed to be happy on this earth was take a deep breath and be part of it. A lizard stared at me from his perch on an exposed root, while a scorpion—his poison tail pinched like links of sausage—scurried under a rock. A quick breeze blew dust into a tiny tornado that swirled and vanished.

I stepped onto the rock ledge, then climbed my favorite live oak, which reached over the edge of the cliff. I wrapped my legs around the limb and felt the bark press into my thighs. That was a place to force myself to trust. It was God's limb and I knew very little about it, really. The sky was so high above me and the earth so far below. Still the limb held, and I had nothing to do with it.

A huge black bird circled upward from the valley, his

long wings spread wide, though he never flapped his wings. Even so, he rose. He banked the curves in ever widening circles, catching an unseen power that lifted him up. When the bird was well overhead, he broke from his circle and coasted into the distance until he was just a speck against the pale blue sky.

Mother and Eleanor sat on the ledge right beside my limb, close enough to talk.

"Aunt Eleanor," I began. "Do you think that you can stay a nun? Go back to Mr. Gaylord Lewis and . . . well, undo whatever you did? And we can all live here. The three of us and Bunny and maybe even Joe Brewer, if he wants."

Eleanor looked over at me on my low-slung branch. "We just have to be realistic, Ruby Clyde."

Realistic! If I were a realistic person I would have landed in the orphanage back at the Okay Corral, that's where being realistic would have gotten me. I wasn't going to start being realistic now. And frankly, I didn't see any reason to be reasonable.

In time, the sun set orange. The sky blued and grayed and swirled into night. I climbed out of the tree and lay back on the hard rock ledge, next to Mother, and watched as the stars appeared one by one. The constellations told a much different story than back at the crime scene. I saw the twins, side by side in the dark sky; between them twinkled a cowgirl with hat and boots, and a little pig, of course, with a corkscrew tail.

THIRTY-THREE

*B*UT HARMONY DOESN'T STICK, NO MATTER HOW sweet. Life goes up, around, and down. *All good things come to an end,* my mean grandmother used to say, and she always seemed happy to be right about that, like maybe you get points for thinking happiness is stupid.

Joe Brewer showed up late one afternoon, and I knew from his face that he was not happy: a wrinkle between his eyebrows, his smile strained. Before coming inside he gave Bunny a peanut butter dog treat, something he'd taken to keeping in his pocket, which is probably the reason Bunny chased his tail whenever Joe Brewer pulled up in front of the house.

As Bunny munched, Mr. Brewer said to all of us, "We need to talk about the trial."

He seemed worried. Eleanor invited him inside, where he spread his papers on the table. He showed us a witness list that he had received from the prosecutor, that's the lawyer on the other side, the one trying to put Mother in prison.

"There's Jerry Smith, the owner of the Okay Corral. He testified at Carl's trial and that is the place where the robbery took place. I don't believe that he can say anything about Barbara's involvement in the crime. You're sure, Barbara, that you had no idea that Carl was planning to rob the place and that you stayed in or near the car the entire time?"

"She did," I blurted out. "She didn't know anything. She didn't do anything."

"Barbara?" Joe Brewer repeated, wanting her to answer for herself. "Did you do anything that could be construed as helping Carl commit this crime? Anything at all?"

Mother squinted, looking up into her head for the memory of that night. She told him that I walked Bunny out in the bushes, using her panty hose as a leash, and she had stayed in the car until the shooting started. "I had no idea that Carl would do such a fool thing," she said.

"Okay, good," Joe Brewer said, and read the next name from the list. "Gus Luna. Who is Gus Luna?"

My stomach twisted with guilt. I hadn't told Joe Brewer about Gus the gunman. If only ignoring unpleasantries could make them disappear, we'd all be better off.

Mother sighed and said, "Carl was a tumbleweed. He picked up friends everywhere. We met Gus Luna at the campsite."

"And he worked in a doughnut shop, best doughnut cutter in Arkansas," I added. "He gave us a box of dough-nuts."

Joe Brewer asked, "What is he doing on the witness list?"

"I don't know," Mother said. "He's just a man and they had some business in Hot Springs. Ruby Clyde and I went sightseeing."

"He didn't travel with you?" Joe Brewer asked. "He wasn't at the Okay Corral?"

"No," we both said, but I knew Gus would be trouble.

"I have to know everything before trial . . ." Joe Brewer dragged his fingers across his forehead. "Sur-prises in the courtroom can kill you."

So I took a deep breath and confessed that it was Gus Luna who had gotten that gun for the Catfish and that we had used it to steal Bunny from the IQ Zoo.

Joe Brewer drew his lips into a tight little knot and finally said, "So that explains the next name. It's the owner of the IQ Zoo in Hot Springs, Arkansas."

"That man! He was torturing Bunny..." Bunny backed up and grunted in disgust. The Circus God from the IQ Zoo was a horrid memory.

But Joe Brewer raised his hand to stop both of us. "We will sort this out later. Right now we have a bigger problem."

We all waited. I thought the problems he had just described were plenty big.

He took a long breath and said slowly, "Carl is also on the witness list."

What? The Catfish again.

"But he's already gone to prison," Eleanor cried. "What could he possibly say?"

Mother shook her head and said, "Carl always has plenty to say."

Joe Brewer explained that he had already brought a motion before the court to prevent Carl from testifying.

But the judge had denied the motion and Joe Brewer did not like that. He sensed the judge would be leaning against us during the trial. Jurors looked to the judge for guidance, every little smirk and smile could influence them. And what's worse, Joe Brewer explained, the Catfish had made a plea bargain, which meant that if he testified against my mother, his fifteen-year prison sentence would be reduced by five years.

"That's not fair!" I shouted. "He'd betray Mother for a crummy five years." I'd thought the Catfish was gone from our lives for good, but here he came worse than before. Would we never be free of him?

"Happens all the time," Joe Brewer said. "The prosecutor would rather send two people to jail than one. It makes them look good. And if that means reducing one sentence, then so be it. Everybody knows it, and nobody cares."

"Is all lost?" Mother asked.

Joe Brewer looked straight into her eyes and said, "I can't lie to you. This is bad. If they believe him, then it would be direct evidence. But all is never lost."

THIRTY-FOUR

ONE EVENING, NOT LONG AFTER THE BAD NEWS, Eleanor called me down to the front room. I left Bunny by the bed. The stairs weren't so easy for him anymore, all that growing. Once a day was plenty. I scampered down the stairs in my blue balloon pajamas.

Eleanor and Mother wanted to talk to me, she said. I sat on a stool facing them. They sat on the leather sofa looking at me.

Finally Eleanor said, "Ruby Clyde, this is going to seem exceedingly strange to you."

Strange didn't bother me, I thought. What could be stranger than my entire life? I waited.

Eleanor lifted a stack of papers that was beside her on the sofa.

She cleared her throat and said, "Your mother and I have been worried about what is to become of you."

I knew that—nothing strange there. What was to become of me was the first thing I worried about every morning.

"Joe Brewer has informed us that it is possible that Barbara will go to prison for ten years. That means that you will be without a mother until you are twenty-two years old."

Mother took over the conversation and said, "We have a plan."

Silence.

"Does anybody want to tell me this plan?" I asked.

"Eleanor is going to adopt you," Mother blurted.

Okay, that was strange.

"We know this is sudden, Ruby Clyde." Mother took the papers from Eleanor's hands and held them up for me to see. "But we are running out of time. And if they put me back in jail . . ."

"But they won't," I said. "You're innocent."

And then I remembered what Mother had said back in the jail, the first time I saw her after the robbery. She hadn't wanted me then, and she still didn't.

"Fine, just give me away, if that's what you want to do," I said. And the weirdest thing was that I didn't mind being owned by Eleanor Rose, but I didn't want Mother to give me away.

"Listen to the whole plan, Ruby Clyde," Eleanor said.

Mother and Eleanor Rose looked at each other, then Eleanor Rose leaned toward me, took my hand, and said, "There's more. First, the three of us are going into family court and arrange this adoption. Then your mother and I are going to swap places. So if anybody had to go to prison it would be me."

Holy cow! Holy Longhorn cow!

They were going to swap places. Mother and Eleanor Rose. Mother would put on Eleanor Rose's nun habit, and Eleanor Rose would put on Mother's dress and . . . if anybody went to jail it would be Aunt Eleanor.

"Wait a minute!" I yelled. "She can't wear your habit. Don't you have to give it back?"

"I can take my time," she said. And when I looked back and forth between Mother and Eleanor I saw they were dead serious.

"Your brains have walked right out the door and floated away into the clouds."

I stomped upstairs, closed the door, and threw myself into bed. I leaned over the edge to speak to Bunny on the floor. "Oh, pig of mine, we are living in a monkey house and they are throwing bananas at us." He pointed his piggy eyes at me as if this was old news.

The sisters followed me upstairs and sat on my bed. Holding my hands. Crowding me.

"No!" I said. "I can't choose between you."

That's when Eleanor took my chin in her hand and made me look her in the eye.

"Ruby Clyde," she said. "This is not your decision. It is mine. You are the child and I am the adult. This is my life. No matter what you say, I will not change my mind. So don't ever look back on this day and think it was your decision."

She explained her plan, step by step, and told me exactly what she expected me to do.

"But you'll get caught," I said. I had questions and I expected to get answers. I had given the criminal-minded twins control of my life, and this was what they did. I wasn't going to make that mistake again.

They had thought it all out. Nobody else knew they were identical twins except Joe Brewer, because the way they dressed disguised that fact. Mother in her summer dresses and newly short hair. Eleanor who hid her newly grown stubble under her nun's wimple. It would be easy to swap clothes.

"What about your cancer?"

Mother explained that nobody had done a medical exam yet. If she was convicted, they would do an intake exam at the women's prison over in Mountain View. A strip search, she called it. I thought that would be pretty embarrassing, to get naked and be searched by strangers.

Other than the cancer, she said, they were identical.

"Not the fingerprints," Eleanor reminded her. "We are not exactly 100 percent identical. But Joe Brewer told them that the fingerprints they took of Barbara when they booked her in the jail are just filed in a national database. If they fingerprint again at Mountain View Prison it will also be uploaded to a database of millions of fingerprints. Nobody is ever likely to pull them out and compare every little sworl. So long as neither of us gets *arrested*."

She turned her eyes to Mother as if to say that she expected Mother to never get arrested again.

They were going to practice swapping places beforehand. They would go to the clinic and family court. If they pulled off the adoption, then they would swap places for the trial.

"Is Joe Brewer okay with this?" I couldn't believe that a man like that would ever agree to their scheme.

"He hasn't been *told*, if you know what I mean," Mother said.

"It's called plausible deniability," Eleanor said.

Deniability was a Wordly Wizard word, but I didn't shout it out. We weren't speaking the same language anymore. We were living in the Tower of Babel.

"He loves you, Ruby Clyde," Mother said.

"If you can't handle this," Eleanor said, "tell us right now. Because if you ever tell, we all go down. It is the

only thing you have to do. Keep your mouth shut forever."

She knew that was not an easy thing to ask of me. My
mouth was one of my best weapons. But if it meant keeping the ones I loved safe, then I could lock my lips closed
for the rest of my life.

THIRTY-FIVE

OTHER AND ELEANOR WEREN'T NERVOUS. They'd swapped places all the time when they were little, so they weren't worried. "Like riding a bike," Eleanor said. "You never forget."

They'd go to the medical clinic as each other. Eleanor was going to dress like Mother, and go back to the clinic where I had gotten my school shots. She would tell them that she had some indigestion or something. She would also tell them all about her cancer surgery and treatments in another state. Since they were a walk-in clinic they wouldn't insist on getting all the records—after all, she just had indigestion. But she would make them write it down. Eleanor wanted to establish an in-state medical record of her cancer, just in case she went to prison and somebody said, "Hey wait, nobody said you have cancer!"

When I saw them in each other's clothes for the first time, I didn't think they'd fool anybody. Sure, Mother looked like a nun in Eleanor's habit, with just her little face stuck out. Sure, Eleanor wore Mother's dress and her hair had grown back, much like Mother's chopped-off hair. But any fool would see the difference.

Wouldn't they?

Apparently not.

....•••••●•••••••...

THEY WOULDN'T LET ME GO INTO THE CLINIC WITH THEM; they thought I would blow it. Now that's insulting. If there's one thing I'm very good at, it is not blowing my cover.

But I agreed and spent the afternoon with Joe Brewer. We sat by a fountain in the park.

"Tell me again," Joe Brewer asked, "about the IQ Zoo."

I launched off. "It was this bully boy, stupid stupid

bully, you should have seen him in his stupid circus out-fit and a cigarette. Only stupid people smoke cigarettes."

Joe interrupted me. "Ruby Clyde, do you realize how often you use the word *stupid*?"

"So," I said. "It's a strong word. It feels good when I say it."

"But it feels bad when others hear it. And you are better than that."

"What's a better word?"

"I don't know, but I'm sure that a girl who loves vo-cabulary words as much as you do will figure it out. Now, tell me the story without using the word *stupid*, not even once."

I did. It wasn't easy but I did not say the word out loud, but I thought about it a few times.

"Oh, girl. That story is unbelievable. Thank God you are safe." Joe laughed and rubbed his hands over both eyes. "Did the owner see you?"

"Absolutely," I said. "The—whatever you want to call him—circus teenager meanie kid picked me up and threw me out on the sidewalk."

We sat quietly for a moment before he said, "We need to talk about your presence at the trial."

"I have to be there," I said. "We even bought a dress."

"I don't want anybody recognizing you in court. It might be a distraction."

"I still don't know why you won't call me as a witness your own self. I could tell them everything."

"It's complicated, Ruby Clyde. You're a child. You'd say anything for your mother."

"Not so, I wouldn't lie," I said. But I would lie. It was a lie that I wouldn't lie. But I wouldn't have to lie—it was all the Catfish.

"I can't put you on the stand, Ruby Clyde. And if the prosecutor knows about you, she wouldn't either. Child witnesses are too unpredictable and sympathetic."

"At least let me be in the courtroom, please," I said. "Nobody has ever seen me in a dress and hair bow, that's for sure."

"We'll see," he said. "But you will have to trust me."

I fell silent. He didn't press.

Finally I said, "I never trusted my mean grandmother, never. I learned a lot from her. My mother? Well, trust is not the word. I love her, but . . . I don't *not* trust her. And I know she loves me."

"I'm glad you know that." Joe Brewer nodded.

I sighed. "I've always found pieces of people to love. I guess trust is the same way, you have to do it in pieces."

"Trust in pieces. Not bad, Ruby Clyde. Trust in pieces."

Speaking of trust, I had not forgotten my bargain with God. Aunt Eleanor had lived and I needed to do something important for her.

I reached in the plastic bag I'd brought and scattered bread crumbs, and in just a few seconds we were surrounded by a swarm of pigeons pecking, bobbing, and flapping.

"Joe Brewer," I said. "I need your help."

"Anything," he said.

"There's one thing I can't do for myself."

"There's a whole lot of things you can't do for yourself, Ruby Clyde."

"Yeah, yeah," I waved him off. "I'm serious. You know I told you about Eleanor's son, the one she gave up for adoption."

He got respectful and said, "Yes, of course."

The mist from the fountain blew across my arm, making the hairs stand up.

"Can you find her son?" I tossed another handful of

crumbs into the middle of the flock, and they darted madly, stupidly, seeking bread.

"I don't know. Breaking adoption records is difficult." Joe squinted at the gray birds scratching in the dirt, at their beautifully shaped heads and deep black pearls for eyes.

I told him everything Eleanor had told me, when and where she had her son. "So why can't you just call them? It will be easy."

"Nothing's easy," Joe Brewer said. "You should know that by now. But I can try. Especially since Sister Eleanor is . . . not well."

I wondered if he had almost said *dying*. Eleanor had insisted that not all people with cancer die, but she was certainly training us to get along without her.

"You don't sound very . . . hopeful." I hesitated because I needed him to have hope about everything.

"Oh, girl, I live on hope. All defense lawyers do." He reached into the bag and threw a handful of bread bits to one side of the pigeons. The shiny gray birds wheeled and bobbed as one, and sucked up the crumbs like a vacuum cleaner.

THIRTY-SIX

*T*HEN CAME FAMILY COURT. IF WE GOT CAUGHT there I didn't know what would happen. Still, they were determined to try it—change my legal guardian from Mother to Eleanor. Only Mother would be Eleanor, and Eleanor would be Mother, so we weren't really changing anything. I was losing track of reality fast.

My confusion was complete. The adults were going to do what they were going to do. They were in complete control and I had no choice but to trust them, dangerous or not.

Eleanor and I wore the matching mother-daughter dresses. That dress I hate to this day. It's amazing how the wrong clothes can make you feel stupid—I mean awkward. Mother clipped that silly bow in my hair and I let her. I negotiated keeping my boots for that bow. My cowboy boots were getting snug, but I wore them anyway.

Mother put on Eleanor's nun habit and her big heavy glasses.

We headed out in the blue van first thing in the morning, Mother driving. Eleanor directed us to the court. "Don't say anything," they kept peppering me. "Only speak if you are spoken to, only if the judge asks you a direct question. Then keep your answer simple."

It was like they all thought I was . . . a child, which I was, but I knew how to handle myself, better than they did. You wouldn't catch me swapping places and walking into a courtroom, that's for sure.

We parked.

Joe Brewer wanted us to meet him in the hall outside of family court. It was not the place where Mother's criminal trial would be held, he said. Another building nearby.

If he knew what they were up to, he never let on.

The adults stood in the hall talking, while I waited near the big window, feeling the sun slanting across my face. I wasn't afraid, not really. So many things had gone wrong that the edge of fear had slipped from my life.

When it was time for court, the adults pushed through the swinging doors, into the courtroom, and I followed. It was my first courtroom ever. I stopped in the aisle, looking at a huge lady statue in the corner—she was blindfolded, and carried a sword in one hand, and in the other hand she balanced a couple of plates on strings. "Lady Justice" she was called, standing there in court—a place dedicated to finding truth and justice, as Joe Brewer said. I certainly hoped that Lady Justice stayed blindfolded and that she didn't see our truth that day, because we were telling big fat lies.

We stood up. A judge, who looked like somebody's grandmother, came in and sat. We sat back down but not for long.

We were first on the docket, Joe Brewer said. A docket is the list of people coming to court. We walked to the judge's desk and looked up at her. They sit up high, judges do. I stood, with exceptionally good posture, between

Eleanor and Mother, holding both of their hands. Joe Brewer talked the talk. Custody, conservatorship, adoption. I don't know what all they did legally to take me from my mother and give me to Eleanor—only, as I have said, they were giving me to my mother, who had me already.

I kept an eye on Lady Justice, daring her to peek out from behind that blindfold.

But since everybody was in agreement, it was fast and simple. After looking at all the papers and listening to Joe Brewer explain what he called the circumstances, the judge leaned over her desk and spoke.

"I want to commend you, Mrs. Henderson, for this extraordinary step you are taking. Considering your medical and legal problems, you are putting the interests of your child ahead of your own. I must say, we don't see that very often in family court."

Eleanor, as Mother, said, "Thank you very much, your honor. I know my sister will love Ruby Clyde as her own."

And it was done.

...........•••••........

IT TOOK ME ALL SUMMER AND INTO THE FIRST OF school to finally finish reading the original, long version of *Oliver Twist*. That boy! He'd gotten into more trouble than I had, but he survived. It always annoyed me that Oliver Twist never did much for himself, he just went along with whoever had him: the child farm, the workhouse, the horrible coffin-builder Mrs. Sowerberry, and that criminal pickpocket Fagin.

Well, once he ran away. That was action. But the Maylies and Mr. Brownlow had to rescue him, and Oliver Twist hadn't done *anything* himself—they just caught him and took care of him. Oliver Twist was lucky more than anything.

What the book showed me most was that you need to be careful who you fall in with. They can get you in big-time trouble. Fagin was a mastermind criminal with a band of children pickpockets, very funny, but bad. Yet the Artful Dodger (and I admit I'm more of an Artful Dodger than an Oliver Twist) only hurt himself by staying with Fagin. Don't even get me started on that wicked Bill Sykes! Why would a nice lady like Nancy stay with him? Like Mother staying with the Catfish. Bill Sykes killed Nancy dead, and I'm just glad that didn't happen to Mother.

Mr. Bumble, Mrs. Sowerberry, Fagin. All bad. You have to find the Maylies and the Brownlows in this life and hang on as best you can.

I had found my people there on Paradise Ranch, and while I had doubted they could fool the family court, they had. And they'd done it for me.

Toward the end of *Oliver Twist*, I read:

> *And now, the hand that traces these words,*
> *falters, as it approaches the conclusion of its*
> *task; and would weave, for a little longer space,*
> *the thread of these adventures.*

Mr. Charles Dickens didn't want the story to be over. I must admit that I wanted the *Adventures of Oliver Twist* to go on. I wanted to read more, and more. But not so for my own adventures. I was ready for the misadventures of Ruby Clyde to fast-forward. I wanted a happy ending of my own and I wanted it fast.

THIRTY-SEVEN

SCHOOL STARTED AND I WAS DOING WELL ENOUGH, but I hadn't made any friends. I hadn't really needed any since I got Bunny, but he couldn't come to school with me. He'd taken to spending his days at the Red Eye with Frank. We'd drop him off in the morning and pick him up after school. And let me tell you, it was no small feat convincing the pig to ride with my mother driving the blue van, but I'd sit in the back with my hand over his eyes the whole time.

There were a couple of bullies at school, and you know how I feel about bullies, I used to beat them up, easy—but I'd grown up. My boots were even making blisters on my heels. Also, I feared that if I caused any trouble, some-body might discover our secrets. So I trained my mind away from the little idiots.

One day Joe Brewer showed up at my school to have lunch with me. I'd seen other kids with adult visitors, mostly parents, but I never asked Mother or Eleanor to come because, well . . . our secret again.

I couldn't stop smiling that I had a guest at school. Even though the other students had been cruel to me, because word got around about my mother being arrested for armed robbery, I didn't care. They were staring at me wondering who this big important man was, having lunch with me, Ruby Clyde Henderson. (I was also glad that we had graduated up to the full-sized table and chairs. I didn't think it would be appropriate for a man like Mr. Joe Brewer to sit down in one of those little chairs they had in the lower school. His knees would be up around his ears.)

A timid boy approached our table, shoulders up, and asked, "Is that your daddy?"

Joe Brewer, as my daddy, was too much to hope for, and I so wanted to say yes, because he could be my daddy. He could. But I shook my head, no.

The kid rocked back and forth on his heels. "They bet he was a policeman coming to arrest you. I bet that he was your daddy. Damn."

"Watch your language, young man." Joe Brewer stood up and waited for the boy to slink back to his tableful of snickering weasels.

Joe Brewer sat back down slowly and cocked his head. I shook my head that it didn't matter. I'd mastered that since the first week of school, when the bullying started. I didn't care, not one little titch. Really I didn't.

"Have you spoken to a teacher about all this?" Joe Brewer sized up the situation all by himself.

I said no, I could handle it. Actually, I had spoken already to the homeroom teacher, but she just said not to come whining to her. She said I needed to get a backbone. If she only knew! I tell you what, I had a much bigger backbone than she would ever have. I could beat her to pieces with my backbone. I had plenty of backbone. Ask anybody. Except that teacher, of course. She was— I bit my tongue at the "S" word and instead said *wrong-headed*. Who on earth would tell a child to get a backbone?

After we finished eating, Joe Brewer asked me to get

my book bag and come out to the car. On the way out, he stopped at the teachers' table and said to all of them, "I am taking Ruby Clyde Henderson home for the afternoon. When she returns in the morning I expect you to have taught your students and yourselves a lesson in civics. The law of this land is *innocent until proven guilty.*"

They stared up at him like raccoons caught in the garbage.

He continued. "I am an officer of the court and I have the power to provide a guard for her safety."

Then I piped up, "And armed guards won't look too good for your school."

Joe Brewer took me by the elbow and marched me out. "We've made our point."

I didn't make any friends at school, but after that, they gave me a wide berth.

••••••••••••••••••••

ANYWAY, ON THE DRIVE BACK TO THE RANCH, AFTER WE picked up Bunny from the Red Eye, Joe Brewer announced he had a surprise for me. He rolled up to the ranch house and stopped, then broke into the biggest smile I'd ever seen on his face. He was usually a grinner, not a toothy smiler.

I turned in the car seat and waited.

He reached into his jacket pocket and took out an envelope. "I received this letter from the home for unwed mothers."

He'd done it. He'd found Eleanor's son. And he must have gotten good news because his pride was busting out.

"Why don't you do the honors," he said, handing me the envelope.

I turned it over in my hand. Then I showed it to Bunny and said, "I thought something so important would be bigger, heavier—too heavy to lift. Like you."

We got out of the car. Bunny twirled by Joe Brewer, waiting for his treat. I headed toward the porch. Eleanor was looking out the window. She had no idea what we were about to tell her. Life is like that. Full of surprises.

Eleanor walked onto the porch and saw us, obviously in cahoots. "What are you three up to now?"

We walked up the stairs of the porch.

"What?" she asked. Suspicious.

"I hope you don't mind, Sister Eleanor . . ." Joe Brewer started. And he explained how I had wanted to give her peace of mind about her son. He explained how he had finally located the home for unwed mothers and spoken to the administrator at length. At first there was a wall of privacy, he said. But he explained to the administrator that the birth mother had a life-threatening illness and that she needed to know that she did the right thing by her son. No details, just assurance that the child was safe and well and loved.

"I used all of my trial techniques, my powers of persuasion," he smiled. "But she refused, citing the strict privacy policies that were agreed upon at birth. It was in the child's best interest, she said, and warned me never to call again. But then out of the blue I received this in an envelope with no return address."

Aunt Eleanor took the envelope, unfolded the paper, and read. Her eyebrows arched high into her forehead, making her eyes round and wide. They filled with tears that spilled down her cheeks. She caught a quick breath and said, "Oh dear God."

We sat quietly. Mother joined us on the porch and

Eleanor said, "Look at this, Barbara. Look what your daughter has done."

She handed Mother the letter. Mother read it and handed it back to Eleanor. From her face I couldn't tell if Eleanor was happy or sad. Finally she asked me, "Have you read this?"

I shook my head.

"Do you want to?" she asked.

I nodded.

She handed me the letter and said, "After all, this is your doing."

I unfolded the paper; it was a handwritten letter.

Dear biological birth mother,

I've always known I was adopted so I don't mind writing you a letter. I have other siblings who are also adopted. I'm not supposed to say anything about them or us or me. But I am happy with my mom and dad, and I do have everything I want, except a skateboard. Mom won't let me.... Wait, I can't say that either. I have a nice house and friends and stuff and I'm healthy. They said you wanted to know that. Thank you for asking. I can't sign my name, but I have one.

Bye,

·········●·········

I WENT UPSTAIRS TO REST. RAIN FELL SOFTLY ON THE roof. I drifted into sleep with my light on, imagining that the rain was tears of angels crying for Eleanor and her son. When I woke up, it was night. My bedside light was on. But Eleanor sat on the edge of my bed, holding my hand.

"Hi," she whispered.

"Hi," I whispered back. "I hope you don't mind I did that. I needed to do something important for you. I promised God."

"I do not mind." She squeezed my hand. "And I wouldn't recommend breaking promises to God."

"That's good."

"It's like your pieces of love," she said. "You have given me a piece of the child I can never fully know."

"But I wanted to heal your cancer."

"Ruby Clyde." She lifted my hand and kissed the fingers. "Listen to me. You have healed something far more important." She took my hand and held it over her heart, and we sat like that for a long time. I leaned into her, then she kissed the top of my head and said, "My son is where he is supposed to be, and you, child, are here with me."

Then she reached over my head and switched off the bedside lamp.

That night, in my dreams, I grabbed snakes right behind their heads and looked in their mouths. But I wasn't afraid because I could see all the way down their throats to their empty rattles.

THIRTY-EIGHT

E HAD MADE A PLAN TO LEAVE PARADISE Ranch before Mother's trial. It wasn't safe for Mother to pretend to be Eleanor in the Hill Country; certainly the nuns would catch on. Eleanor had said her goodbyes. In their minds, Eleanor had quit being a nun and would take care of me elsewhere. Before the trial, we would pack bags and be prepared to stay in town with Joe Brewer. I still held out hope that we might win in court, but if we lost then Mother and I would live in town. But I would lose Eleanor.

Bunny had to be cared for. Frank had agreed, happily, to take him. It was the right thing to do. I couldn't keep him. Like Eleanor giving up her son, I had to do what was best for my pig. He couldn't live in a high-rise or a city or wherever we ended up in life. He deserved better, and that meant living with Frank.

The day before Mother's trial, I took my pig to the Red Eye. Frank was pumping gas when we came up the road. I walked over with a big smile on my face. *Act as if, and the feelings will follow.* My mean grandmother always said that, and she was right sometimes. But I wasn't nearly as happy as the smile on my face. Still, it kept me from crying.

"Bunny!" Frank hooked the nozzle back and swung her big arm. "Come see what I built you, my friend."

Right beside the building, under the big bloodshot eyeball, she had made a pen with a trough for food. It had a hose to fill the water bucket and she had made Bunny a big sloppy mud puddle. He was much too big for me to pick up anymore, so I kneeled down beside him and wrapped both arms around his neck. Our hearts beat together for a few brief moments, then I let go and stood up. Bunny waddled into his new pen and rolled over in the mud, as happy as I had ever seen him.

Frank propped the gate open with a cinder block. "He's

smart enough to roam free. I'll just tuck him in at night to keep him safe. Is that okay with you, Ruby Clyde?"

I handed Frank the $257.

"What's this, Sugar Foot?"

"Some I had, most I made here washing trucks; I want you to have it."

She was about to refuse, but I pushed on. "I'm a girl who needs to *do* things. You're taking my pig for me, and I want you to have this money. Spend it on him if you wish, but just take it. Please."

She did.

And that is how I left my pig. Under the big eye that had seen that whole part of my life, one that I would shortly leave behind. Bunny. Living at the Red Eye Truck Stop, where he would spend the rest of his days lolling in the mud by Frank's door and winking at cowboys who stopped for gas or food. No Cadillac, no bacon. Life had worked out for Circus God's pig.

·······•·•······

THAT AFTERNOON, I ASKED ELEANOR WHAT WOULD happen if Mother were not found guilty at trial. "You all seem so sure that we will lose. What if Mother doesn't lose and you don't have to go to prison?"

She said, "That, dear child, would be a delightful problem."

"And if you go to prison, what will you do?"

"I will minister to the incarcerated women," she said, as if she had given that much thought. "It is not often that we are given the opportunity to make a true sacrifice. You know, Ruby Clyde, people argue about the Bible all the time, making it serve their own agendas, but one thing is perfectly clear. Jesus got up on that cross. And instead of getting on a cross for others, we run around saying Jesus died for me, me, me, but that's a bit selfish, don't you think?"

"Can I visit you in prison?" I bypassed the Bible lesson because I was missing her already.

She laughed gently. "I don't know. I'm going to be pretty busy at my new calling."

"I'm serious. I want to see you."

"We can write letters and talk on the telephone, but I think you've seen enough of the legal system for a lifetime."

I started to cry. There was nothing left in me to hold back the tears.

"Tears are good, baby. You don't need to visit on my account, truly. If you really need to see me, then Joe Brewer can bring you. But I deeply hope that you will be busy with the new life we have worked so hard to give you."

Later, Mother and I rocked on the front porch and then she tucked me into bed, but I couldn't sleep. It was a moonless night so my room was pitch-black dark. No matter how wide I opened my eyes, it was a wall of black. And my mind wouldn't stop. What if, what if, what if . . .

Finally I got out of bed and tiptoed into Aunt Eleanor's room. I knew it might be a very long time before we were together again. I slipped in beside her and snuggled up close to her back and tried to breathe with her. She stirred, saw that I was there with her, then adjusted the bedding to cover me up. She didn't seem worried at all. So I decided not to worry either.

All good things come to an end, my mean grandmother always said. But you know what? All bad things come to an end too.

THIRTY-NINE

*T*HE DAY FINALLY CAME FOR THE TRIAL.

Eleanor (dressed as Mother in that matching dress) pushed through the swinging doors, into the courtroom, with Joe Brewer beside her. Mother (dressed in Eleanor's habit and wimple) followed with me (in my silly dress) holding her hand. I knew they had practiced swapping places, but I was nervous. This was a trial for Mother's freedom. Anything could happen. What if they both ended up in prison?

I stopped cold and stood there looking at Law Itself. The big seal of Texas on the wall. Flags on either side of a big raised desk for the judge. His hammer was sitting there waiting for him. Guards, policemen, and people in suits all seemed at home, standing around chatting.

Joe and Eleanor took their places at the defense table up front.

Mother and I sat in the front row behind them, feeling miserable. *Miserable* is the only word that describes what I felt, sitting in that courtroom not knowing anything about anything. Being ignorant is a feeling I do not like. And my dress and hair bow weren't helping. Much less those new sneakers I had to wear. I had a tan line from wearing my boots all summer so my white ankles looked pathetic.

A man up front announced, "All rise."

We all rose.

The judge walked in wearing a long black dress. He was short and his neck was skinny. Actually, he looked like Mr. Potato Head. When he sat down behind that big high desk, the rest of us sat down too. Judge Potato Head was mumbling into his microphone about calendars and who needed what and when and where.

Finally the judge said, "Mr. Brewer, are you ready to bring the juror pool in?"

I pictured the jurors all swimming in circles, like those *synchronized* (*Wordly Wizard,* shouted in my head) swimmers in flowery plastic caps.

"Yes, your honor," Joe Brewer said. "If it please the court."

Why should it not please the court, I thought. Wasn't that why we were all there? What if the judge said, *Now that you ask, it does not please the court?*

"Are you ready, A.D.A. Barber?"

I later learned that stood for Assistant District Attorney Barber. But I heard *Aging Barbie,* and that is exactly what she looked like. An old-lady doll with blond hair flowing out in all directions. Aging Barbie wore a tight purple skirt and pointy heels so high she looked like a toe dancer.

The judge ordered the bailiff to bring in the potential jurors.

In marched about 150 people, and they crowded the rows. Judge Potato Head asked them some general questions about their health and stuff. Then the lawyers started spraying them with questions. The attorneys tried to guess which jurors would be on their side by asking things like which magazines they read. Joe Brewer had a kind voice, but Aging Barbie spoke like a machine, fast and monotone. Rat-a-tat-tat. She did this kind of thing all day every day. Send people to jail. What a job.

You should have seen the jurors they ended up with. Twelve of them, plus two extras in case somebody fell out. There were some men and some women, white, brown, and one who was bluish green. And every one of them was a big-shouldered person. They made the jury box look kind of crowded.

Joe Brewer was right. They never put my name on a witness list, so I could stay in the courtroom during the trial. I was glad. If they made me sit outside, I would have died of curiosity and anxiety and aloneness. Besides, I was sure that watching real hard would help us win. Still I worried one of the witnesses might see me and make trouble.

Aging Barbie stood up on those high heels and explained about all the people she had found to testify against my mother, and she was just absolutely certain, beyond a shadow of a doubt, that anybody with an ounce of common sense would see that Barbara Henderson was guilty as charged. That lady was wrong, again. I had a pound of common sense, but common sense was not all it's cracked up to be.

Joe Brewer stood up and said just the opposite. Barbara Henderson was innocent until proven guilty and the State had no credible evidence, "No leg to stand on." He threw out his chin in absolute certainty.

First witness up was Gus Luna. It was a long ways to come from Arkansas, but coming to court must have made him feel important. And a man like Gus Luna didn't have much opportunity to feel important, other than being the best doughnut cutter in Arkansas.

He said, "That woman gave her boyfriend the money to buy her that gun." That was *so* not true. Gus Luna was a big fat liar. But I was happy that he pointed right at Eleanor when he said *that woman*, even though her hair was chopped off. They had tricked him.

What's more, that fool looked right at me in the courtroom, but he didn't recognize me, sitting there in that silly dress and bow. Not the Ruby Clyde he had seen back in Hot Springs, that's for sure. That gave me a little confidence that I would be invisible for the rest of the trial.

Then Aging Barbie, in her tight purple skirt, brought the Circus God from the IQ Zoo to testify. The jury smiled when he spoke. That surprised me. I guess he was pretty successful in show business, what with his daily performances at the IQ Zoo. He knew how to talk to people. Come to think of it, the jurors looked just like the people who had been in the IQ Zoo watching his Noah's Ark show. Circus God told the jurors that my mother had threatened his entire family and all of his guests and that she was the most violent woman he had ever seen.

Not a word of that was true; he was just embarrassed that we freed his pig. Some people can't stand to be wrong.

All at once the Circus God blurted out, "And what kind of woman gets her son involved in a pig robbery?"

I liked to died. Jittered up my neck to the back of my ears.

"Objection!" Joe Brewer leaped to his feet. "The defendant has no son. And if she did it would be irrelevant to the case at hand."

"Sustained," the judge said. And that meant it was okay, but I still felt sickish.

Then old Jerry Smith, the owner of the Okay Corral Gas and Food Mart, sat up there by the judge and told everybody what had happened when the Catfish came into his store. I wasn't worried even a titch because he had never seen me. Old Jerry Smith said he was up at the cash register by himself, counting out the coins and putting them into bank bags. He was sipping on a cold beer when in walks the Catfish. Jerry didn't think there was going to be trouble because the Catfish was friendly and scrawny, so Jerry went back to counting. The Catfish strolled up and down every single aisle, picking up one product from each one: motor oil, Q-tips, pork rinds, and a cigarette lighter. Finally, Catfish marched up to Jerry Smith at the cash register and said, "You got any fresh fruit?" Then he pointed the gun at old Jerry's face, smiled, and cackled, "Fruit-cake." Which made no sense at all, but Jerry got the idea he was being robbed.

Then he pointed a finger at Eleanor. "And that woman helped him." He bought it too. Whew.

Judge Potato Head laughed and shook his head like maybe what Old Jerry had said was funny. The jury looked at him, then shook their heads and smiled. I saw what Joe Brewer meant. That judge had an attitude and the jury was catching it like a virus.

Aging Barbie then called her last witness: the Catfish, in all his whiskered glory. Shameless, he looked around the room like he was walking onstage. Some kind of policeman escorted him to the witness stand. He swore on the Bible, sat down, and eyeballed the courtroom some more.

His gaze hung on "Eleanor," and he looked surprised and sad at her short hair. He didn't seem to notice that Mother and Eleanor had swapped places. Whew.

But he found me in the first row—glanced at the nun, and then locked eyes with me. I could see the machinery in his mind. The nun in her habit (the one we had talked about in the car), me looking like a girly fool, and the damning testimony he was about to give against my mother. I held my breath, wondering if he was going to call me out.

He looked unhappy for just a flash, then he wiggled, and right up there in front of God and country, he said that my mother had asked him to steal the pig (which was true) and lied that she had ordered him to rob the Okay Corral because she didn't want to ask her sister for a place to stay (which was so *not* true).

I about came out of my seat. Selling Mother down the creek, for five crummy years off his sentence. He couldn't look at Mother again after telling those lies but he did look at me. And I tried to kill him with my eyes, he could see that, and he knew he was condemning my mother and leaving me alone in the world, going to an orphanage like he had said on the car ride. What kind of man would do that for five years off the crime he commited himself? A stinky catfish, that's what.

But he wrinkled up his brow and turned away, pulled on his nose like he was about to cry. He had no business being sad, but at least he hadn't mentioned my name. I guess he had one decent bone in his body, but it was extremely well hidden.

Joe Brewer cross-examined the Catfish and asked him if he'd made a deal with the State to reduce his sentence in exchange for his testimony.

"What if I did?" The cocky Catfish slung his elbow

over the back of his chair and stuck out his chest. "I wouldn't lie."

Wouldn't lie? I thought. *Not only does he tell big fat ones, but he gives liars a bad name.*

"And how many times have you been arrested?"

"Objection," shouted Aging Barbie. "Irrelevant."

"Sustained." The judge leaned back in his chair and looked at the ceiling.

Joe Brewer came again with a slightly different question. "How many times have you been in prison?"

"Your honor, *please*," Aging Barbie cried out again. "Move to strike."

"Move along, Mr. Brewer." The judge lowered his face into his hands in complete exasperation.

Joe Brewer argued with Judge Potato Head about what could and couldn't be said in court. And the judge never agreed with him. Some judges are just determined to send everybody to prison.

The Catfish was excused from the stand and was escorted out of the court by that policeman, and that was the last time I saw his sorry self. Good riddance. If I see him in fifteen years, when I am twenty-seven years old,

I might just put a hook in his mouth and use him for bait.

That was the end of witnesses.

Then Aging Barbie did what is called closing argument, where she stood up and said every horrible thing she could think of about my mother. And she finished by saying, "If it looks like a duck, walks like a duck, quacks like a duck, then you have to find that it is a duck." She was getting ducks and facts mixed up, but that didn't bother her one little bit. Joe Brewer got up when it was his turn and did just the opposite. He used his whole body and heart to tell the jurors that Mother was innocent. He convinced me, but I was already on his side.

Then *bang*, went the judge's hammer. "Bailiff, take the jury out now."

..............●..............

"YOU NEED TO PREPARE YOURSELF, RUBY CLYDE. IT IS not going our way." He'd read them all—the judge, the jurors. At least Joe Brewer was telling me the truth, most adults wouldn't have. They would have pumped up a lot of hope words. But he just said it: we were losing.

Sure enough the jury came back two and a half hours later and said Mother was guilty. She would be taken into custody right away, and transported to the Mountain View Prison for Women.

Only it wasn't Mother who was going to Mountain View. Mother was sitting beside me in Eleanor's nun habit, with her little square face and big black glasses. The woman they led out of the courtroom was my aunt Eleanor, former nun, current prisoner for ten long years.

I stood up, perfectly still, with my arms by my sides, watching as they led Aunt Eleanor toward the side door.

She was polite to the guard who took her by the elbow, turned her, and put her in handcuffs. I was afraid that she wouldn't turn back and look at me. She was brave and calm so that meant I had to be brave and calm too, but if she walked out of that courtroom without looking at me, I'd scream my head off. I held my breath and watched.

Just before disappearing into the side room filled with

holding cages for criminals, my aunt Eleanor Rose looked over her shoulder and blew me a kiss.

I felt like we were a piece of paper being torn in two.

Later, one of the jurors told Joe Brewer that it wouldn't have taken that long but they wanted to stay and get the free lunch.

·········●●●·········

WE WERE ALL STUNNED. NO ENTIRE CLUE WHAT TO DO with ourselves.

It was late afternoon. Joe Brewer took us over to the park by the river, there by the bat bridge. It was one of the largest bat colonies in the world, and we were going to watch the bats come out of their sleeping holes under the bridge. It happened every evening.

As the sun went down, the little bodies began to fall out and sail up the river. At first I only saw a few zippy shapes, then I saw more and more and more, until bats swarmed the sky. All the while dark was closing in around us like a fog.

Finally it got so dark I couldn't see the bats, and I

thought maybe they had all come out and gone, but somebody standing on the bridge turned on a big spotlight. Bats were everywhere. They flew through the cone of light like spirits racing from the dead.

"Do they fly back like this in the morning?" I asked.

Joe Brewer said no, they flew home one at a time.

FORTY

E SPENT THE MONTH LIVING WITH JOE Brewer in town, me in my new school and Mother doing some kind of training with Joe Brewer so she could get a job. I was broken in unspeakable ways. Mother was better, but I worried where we would go, or what we would do. I wasn't entirely sure Eleanor had trained Mother enough to take care of me all by herself. I missed Eleanor Rose so much it hurt my heart, the real one beating in my chest.

I often wandered around the apartment pointlessly, trying to be grateful because I knew that was what Eleanor would have wanted. I wanted to please her; after all, I had made that bargain with God, but I didn't recognize the bargain anymore. She was alive, but in prison. What kind of deal was that?

One night I was particularly restless; I had done my homework and gone back to the kitchen to wash the dinner dishes. The hot water on my hands calmed me. I wondered why I had ever thought I had healing hands. Who had I ever healed, really, medically? I couldn't even heal myself into hope. While the water ran, reddening my hands, I told myself that healing takes time.

Joe Brewer came up from behind. He reached over my shoulder and turned the water off. He hugged me.

I wiggled away and walked out to the terrace. He followed me. The constant thought of my Eleanor Rose in prison cut like razors at my heart.

I said, "I thought trusting would make a happy ending. But I didn't know that I would lose Eleanor . . ."

"Trust is stepping into the unknown," he said.

"I do that," I said. "I step into the unknown all the time."

"I know you do. But trust is stepping into the unknown

with another person. Together. Trusting the other to have your back. I have your back."

Joe Brewer took my hand and held it to his heart. We stood looking at the sparkling lights, which were so very beautiful, painfully beautiful.

I realized for the first time that I wasn't dizzy in his apartment anymore. The floor didn't feel like it was swaying beneath my feet. I was on solid ground, sort of. Solid ground up in the sky.

That's when Joe Brewer told me that he had found another place for us to live, a place where Mother and he could both find work and we could start over.

"You're coming with us?" I asked.

Joe Brewer said, "I couldn't control the case, Ruby Clyde. But caring for you is something I have complete control over. You and your mother will never be alone."

"I like that," I said. "And so would Eleanor."

"Yes," he nodded. "She was counting on it. That was part of her plan."

........•○•........

Joe Brewer was moving us to St. Louis. Of course we had to go. We couldn't stay anywhere else in Texas. But I knew that I would keep the Hill Country in my heart forever. Turtles carry their homes with them, why couldn't I? Besides, my home was no longer a place, it was my people. People heal each other, and it takes time.

I was not certain that I knew what to do with a fresh start. Trouble was familiar. Trouble had seemed to be my destiny. I had embraced trouble and survived. A new and unfamiliar life was coming. The gift of a new life— freely given from Eleanor to the three of us—was the last thing I ever expected. Every day would be a gift.

Joe Brewer got a job in St. Louis. St. Joe, he was.

"You'd give up your job here, for us?" I asked, when he first explained it to me. He wasn't giving up anything, he said. He was gaining everything.

"Besides," he spoke slowly as if he were working it out in his head, "I don't feel that I can be an officer of the Texas court any longer. I didn't plan this, but I turned a blind eye and allowed it to happen."

"Are you sorry?" I asked.

"Heavens no! I'd do it again. Listen to me, Ruby. I have given this much thought. Certain people will think that what I have done is wrong. And they would be correct. Other people will think that what I have done is right. And they would also be correct. Sometimes we are faced with impossible choices. And that is life. But I can't stand up in the same Texas court in good conscience, as if nothing has occurred. That would be a lie. We know the truth. We will go forth and build our new life on the truth. I will be like your uncle. Would you like that?"

My uncle? Joe Brewer may not have known it but he would be more than my uncle soon enough. I'd seen his eyes when he looked at Mother. I knew the extra hours he gave us. He'd given up his job. Joe Brewer could say whatever he wanted, but I knew better. I was no fool. And frankly, I liked getting back to knowing more about adults than they knew about themselves.

And wouldn't you know it, even though he'd given up the practice of law in Texas, Joe Brewer could still teach it in Missouri. He had a job teaching legal ethics in

St. Louis and running a clinic for the downtrodden. We'd go there, to St. Louis, and be a family: an uncle, a mother, a little girl.

Joe Brewer had everything in his apartment packed up by professional movers. Mother and I had very little of our own. We left the household items at the ranch for the next nun. Eleanor Rose had few worldly possessions, as she called them, only the books by Charles Dickens, which she wanted me to have and made me promise to read, every one of them.

Nobody was at the ranch on the day we stopped by to pick up the books that Eleanor Rose had insisted we take with us. I lifted them off the shelf one by one, dusting them and placing them in a cardboard box. "Be sure to look at *Oliver Twist* and *A Tale of Two Cities*," she said twice, and she made Joe Brewer promise to remember. "I've left messages for you there," she said.

When I opened *Oliver Twist*, an envelope fell out. Eleanor had written *Barbara* across the front. I picked it up from the floor and shook the book, hoping to find a letter for me. There wasn't one, but Eleanor had written in the front of the book:

Dearest Ruby Clyde,

I have done everything in my power to keep you from being an orphan like Oliver Twist. The rest is up to you.

Love always, E.R.

P.S. When you are ready to have birthdays again, start with A Tale of Two Cities. It is the story of an innocent man who gives his life for someone he loves.

Joe Brewer carried the box of books to the car. I took Mother's letter outside, where she stood on the porch. I handed her the letter from Eleanor Rose. She took it and read it to herself, then she read it to me.

Dearest Barbara,

Please forgive me for shutting you out of my life. We waste our lives for reasons that, looking back, seem so small, so wasteful. We throw out love because it doesn't reach the level of perfection that we demand. At the first pain, we run, but we must walk through pain to find our way back to love.

Love begets love, even if the love is in small flawed pieces.

Ruby Clyde taught me about pieces of love. Let her teach you also.

What happened to that child is enough to bring a grown man to his knees. She will tell you, in time, about hearing the gunshots at the gas station. About being alone under the stars with no hope. She has walked through pain like a tiny soldier. It is time for her to find what's left of her childhood in a peaceful place.

All she has wanted from us was complete love, but we could only give her pieces of it. Maybe pieces of love is all that we can give one another. Maybe pieces of love must be enough for all of us. But it feels like Ruby Clyde has given me more and that is why I gave my freedom for her, my whole love so that she can have a mother.

Can you take care of her now, Barbara, for both of us? Will you?

Your sister, your twin,
Eleanor Rose

My mother lowered the letter and looked at me. "Yes, I can take care of you. I can and I will." Shading her eyes with one hand, she looked out past the peach orchard to the sunlit hill and said, "This is your day, Ruby Clyde."

·········●··········

I AM SITTING IN THE BACKSEAT OF JOE BREWER'S CAR. We are headed east. There's a big wide river in St. Louis—the Mississippi. I crossed it once, when I was asleep, the night Catfish drove us west. I plan to be awake this time to see the water flowing from the north, from towns I have never seen, water swirling in a muddy rush south toward the Gulf of Mexico where it will mix with salt water and spread across the whole entire world.

A Tale of Two Cities (one of the books by Mr. Charles Dickens) is open on my lap. Eleanor Rose wrote in the front: *This is the story of a man who gave his life for love. Please know, Ruby Clyde, that it is a far, far better thing that I do, than I have ever done.*

I turn the pages and read the first lines of the book:

It was the best of times, it was the worst of times . . . it was the season of Darkness, it was <u>the spring of hope</u> . . .

Eleanor underlined those last words—*the spring of hope*. I flip through and see that she underlined many passages and made notes to me in the margins. I close the book and look at the road ahead. In time, I know I will read her pieces of love to me, but not now—later, when I am ready again for birthdays.

ACKNOWLEDGMENTS

THERE IS AN INVISIBLE DAISY CHAIN OF PEOPLE WHO took Ruby Clyde's hand along the path from my imagination to the book you are holding.

I thank each one: Ruby Clyde Henderson for jumping onto my page; the Sewanee Writers' Conference and my workshop leaders Richard Bausch and Jill McCorkle; my friend Rita Bourke and all the past and current members of the Nashville Writers' Alliance; and the independent editor Rebecca Faith, who helped me prepare the manuscript for submission to agents.

A special thanks to the summer intern at MCA, Raven Diltz, who actually pulled Ruby Clyde out of the slush pile and passed her to the team: Maria Carvainis, Bryce Gold, Martha Guzman, and especially the brave and wise Elizabeth Copps, who promptly sold my book to Farrar Straus Giroux.

I have the deepest gratitude for Susan Dobinick and Margaret Ferguson, who saw the heart of the story and freed it from the mess I had given them. And the rest of the FSG team: Kristie Radwilowicz, the cover designer; Karen Ninnis, the copy editor; and Heather Job in publicity.

And the bookseller, librarian, teacher, or friend who brought this book into your life. And finally I thank you for reading it. You are the daisy that makes the entire chain worthwhile.

Thank you one and all. It was not easy, but this perfect daisy chain transformed all the detours, disasters, failures, and frustrations that are unavoidable in this life, especially the creative life.